THE TELL-ALL

LIBBY HOWARD

$\mathcal{I}$'ve mourned my husband twice. Once after the accident that took away the man I'd married. The second time when the stroke took away a man that I'd grown to love—the one who, up until he died, still held random shards of his original self.

Twice. But I'd never had time to mourn the loss of myself until now. How many lives do we go through in the course of one? By my count, I'd had three so far and was beginning my fourth. This fourth, it was the one that scared me the most, the one I felt most unprepared to face. My fourth life—my new life, where there were no clear markers to help me decide my path or the course of my future.

"What do you think I can get for it?" I asked Carson. The words lodged in my throat like boulders that needed to be jackhammered before rising to the surface.

Our home. No, it was *my* home now. Still, the best memories I had were of when it was ours. Every beam and post held a story. They were imbedded deep into the plaster, reminding me of the past—both good and bad. I hated to sell this place.

Maybe it was for the best. The thought of remaining in this house for the rest of my life, waking every morning alone to the same walls that had seen so much…. Let someone else take my place here, meld their own experiences with the thirty-five years of our own.

Though the thought of living somewhere else was just as depressing. More so, actually. Some little apartment where I could hear the footsteps of the tenant upstairs? Escaping the past and launching myself into a new life in a tiny, inexpensive apartment wasn't something I relished. I didn't want to leave. I wasn't ready. But there was a mortgage, and I was painfully aware that I couldn't make the payments—at least not for long. With my new job, I might be able to manage a few months, but after that I'd be on the path to foreclosure. Better for me to list it now and leave with my chin up than be pried from my beloved home by sheriff's deputies and an eviction notice—which would be even more humiliating because I knew those sheriff's deputies. Sell. Like a butterfly emerging from my cocoon, fly free and leave it all behind. And fly away to some cheap, dingy one-bedroom that reeked of old smoke and onions.

I was about to sell my home—*our* home. Lord, how could I ever sell our home?

"Are you sure, Kay?"

Carson had been my friend for decades. The freelance research work that he'd thrown my way over the last ten years had saved me. He'd kept me sane by asking me to do property title searches as well as find copies of deeds, and other documents buried under mounds of courthouse files. Our friendship was more than just the occasional odd bit of work, though. We'd been buddies in college, but after graduation, when we'd gone on to careers and marriage, our camaraderie had turned into more of a couple's friendship with dining out, wine festivals, and charity fundraisers. It was friends like Carson that I cherished—the ones who hadn't abandoned me when I had needed their support the most. His wife, Maggie, had kept me going with casseroles while Carson had provided moral support through those dark years.

"No, I'm not sure. I don't want to leave just yet, but I can't afford to stay here." I winced, hating to tell Carson the sordid details of my finances. "The insurance policy took care of the funeral and the remaining medical bills, but I can't swing the mortgage on my salary."

The house had once been paid off, but after the accident, we'd needed to take out a mortgage to pay the medical bills, then a second mortgage to help pay the first. Then the 401k had been gobbled up with early withdrawals. I was in so far over my head that I doubted I'd clear anything after the sale, even with Carson kindly waving his seller's commission.

"Can you take in some roommates? One or two would cover the mortgage and give you time to think about what you want to do. I hate to see you sell this place, Kay. It's beautiful. It's the house you and Eli had always dreamed of having, the one you both wanted to grow old in."

It had been our dream house—a huge three-story Victorian on a quiet street. I'd fallen in love for the second time in my life the day I saw it. The gingerbread trim, porches, thick wooden baseboards and coffered ceilings—it was magical. It was also too big for two people. We'd intended to fill it with children, but life took another turn and five of the six bedrooms had remained empty. It was too big for two people, and it was definitely too big for one, but I wasn't sure I could expose my raw emotions and precious memories to a roommate who would leave dirty dishes in the sink and muddy shoes on the foyer carpet.

"Look, I know someone who is searching for a place. It's very hush-hush, so I don't want to name any names unless you're interested. He's getting ready to go through a messy divorce and needs somewhere that doesn't look like a bachelor pad so he can push for fifty-fifty custody."

"Please tell me he's not one of the people in that sex scandal?"

That would be the sort of thing that led to a messy divorce. It seemed a Madam—and I mean that with a capital 'M'—had gotten herself arrested earlier this week. Not a big deal unless you considered that Locust Point was a tiny town. That sort of thing would have even been shocking in nearby Milford, but here in Locust Point where everyone knew everyone, it was the topic of every conversation. Caryn Swanson. Attractive, immaculately groomed, party-and-wedding-planner Caryn Swanson. What a scandal.

If having a woman you were likely to run into at the grocery store turn out to be a Madam wasn't enough, there was the juicy speculation on who her clients were. And a Madam meant there were prostitutes. Prostitutes. In Locust Point. We were all eyeing each other, wondering who had been doing a bit of side work with Caryn. But so far the woman kept her lips tightly sealed. No named prostitutes. No incriminating black book. Just a resounding claim of innocence from her lawyer. I had no doubt those coral-pink lips would become unsealed once a plea bargain was on the table.

A Madam in Locust Point meant johns in Locust Point, and I didn't like the idea of having a man who might have solicited prostitutes living in my house.

Carson laughed. In fact, he laughed until I thought he might pass out. "Uh, no. I'm not saying this guy is beyond having an affair—I'm not privy to the details of his divorce. But there's no way that he's getting his loving from prostitutes. No way."

I was willing to take Carson's word for it. But beyond

having a morally bankrupt sex-crazed guy living with me, I had other objections. "He has kids? I'd probably be okay with the occasional overnight, but fifty-fifty custody?"

I hadn't been around kids often in the last ten years, and really not much before that. Our friends tended to be childless, or the type who got babysitters when we all went out to eat.

"They're not infants, Kay. His kids are teens. They'll probably play loud music and spill chips all over their rooms, but you wouldn't have to deal with crying babies, and at most they'd only be here half the time. This place is huge. It's not like you don't have the space. Plus, he's looking for a two-year lease. It would give you money to help with the mortgage, and time to think about what you want to do."

With the rest of my life. It was the unspoken finish to his speech. I didn't care about loud music or snack foods. There wasn't anything two teens could do that two hundred years of families hadn't already done to this house. It was built for more than one person, but could I cope with sharing my home with three strangers after so many years of just Eli and me?

From the corner of my eye I saw a shadow that moved from the back of the kitchen toward the fridge. When I turned to see what it was, the shadow disappeared and I found myself looking at a magnet. It was a picture taken over a decade ago in Costa Rica. Me, waist deep in azure water, pristine white sand in front and a lofty forest-green mountain peak behind. I'm holding some frozen, umbrella-accented drink in the photo and laughing, because it was before the accident. It was before… everything.

The picture blurred, and I wasn't sure if it was the shadow this time, or tears.

I couldn't leave this house. I wasn't ready. I wasn't sure I'd ever be ready. And if that meant I had to put up with some philandering, soon-to-be divorced guy and his two Dorito-eating kids, then so be it. "Thanks, Carson. Please give him my number."

He smiled. "I'll do more than that. Are you free this afternoon? I'll have him come by and meet you."

This was all moving too fast, but that was the way everything had seemed since the funeral. Actually even during the funeral. While I felt as if I were frozen in place, afraid to take a step, the world rushed past me at breakneck speed.

"I have an eye appointment and a few errands. Maybe tonight, or late afternoon? I should be home by three."

Carson typed into his phone. "I'll arrange it. How are your eyes doing? Everything okay?"

Another shadow moved at the edge of my vision. This time I ignored it. "Just a checkup."

It *was* just a checkup, and I wasn't about to tell anyone except my ophthalmologist about the shadows, the movement that I saw in my peripheral vision. I didn't want anyone thinking I was going crazy. I wasn't. I was sure these shadowy figures were just a temporary effect of my cataract surgery, like the weird sparkly light that my friend Daisy told me reflected off the new lenses.

Cataracts, and me just sixty years old. At least I'd been able to scrounge up the money for the surgery. It made things tighter financially, but I'd rather live in a cardboard box on the street than live with the increasingly dark blur of my sight. There were crosses in life I was strong enough to bear, but losing my eyesight wasn't one of them.

Carson's phone beeped, and he glanced down at the screen. "Okay. We're all set. He'll be here at four."

I felt a lump in my chest at the thought. A stranger. Living in my house. And two teenagers. Maybe I'd luck out and he'd hate the place. Although I wasn't sure which option was worse, losing my beloved home, the home that Eli and I had made together, and living in an apartment, or having a stranger in my house every night.

A stranger. I didn't even know who this guy was, if he was a serial killer, or a rapist. A messy divorce didn't give me any confidence that my prospective roomie was an upstanding citizen. I know that was horribly judgmental of me, but as someone who had stuck by her husband through sickness and health, I couldn't help but feel a twinge of annoyance at people who didn't seem to view their marriage vows with the same dedication that I had.

"So, who is this man?" I asked, eyeing my watch. I needed to get going or I'd be late for my eye appointment.

"Judge Beck," Carson said with all the solemn respect of a man announcing the presence of our Lord and Savior. "Judge Nathanial Beck."

CHAPTER 2

" ELOPZD."

"Very nice, Mrs. Carrera."

The doctor smiled at me as if I were a particularly clever child, then proceeded to flash his hand-held light thingy back and forth across each eye.

"The lens attachments look good. Everything has healed nicely." He sat back on his rolling stool, looking for a few seconds as if he had a halo while my eyes adjusted to the room's dim light.

For all I knew, he probably did have a halo. Doctor Berkowitz was a fit man who wore his receding hair trimmed short and had an affinity for t-shirts with quirky sayings on them. Today's shirt proclaimed him to be a Browncoat—whatever that was. He was about my age with warm, friendly eyes in a face whose lines told me he'd spent a lot of his life smiling. Dr. Berkowitz was the type of guy that twenty years ago would have made my heart rate increase, but instead I felt nothing. Zip. Nada. Eli and I had always joked that marriage didn't mean you suddenly went blind. Nor did it mean that ogling an attractive jogger or bartender was a prelude to infidelity. It was normal to see the beauty in other humans around you, and normal to know that the person you married was the only one who truly lit your fire.

But Eli was gone, and the last ten years of our marriage had been challenging. It wasn't just that I couldn't see Doctor Berkowitz as an attractive, eligible man, it was that I couldn't see myself as an attractive, eligible woman anymore. I didn't even recognize the face I saw in the mirror or the body I lathered up in the shower as mine. How had I wound up a young woman in an old body?

How had I wound up a numb robot in an old body?

Not that there was anything beyond professional friendliness in Doctor Berkowitz's demeanor to suggest that he might find me attractive. Not that there had been anything in *anyone's* demeanor in the last ten years to suggest they might find me attractive. I didn't want another man. I wasn't looking for a replacement for Eli or even a weird one-night-stand. It just would be nice if someone would see me as more than an old lady, a childless widow, as more than some androgynous robot. With cataracts. Who saw shadows out of the corner of her eye.

When did I get so old that a good-looking doctor did nothing for me? When did I get so old that a good-looking doctor wasn't eyeing me up with a spark of interest in his own eyes? One day I was looking at forty in the mirror, and the next greeting my sixtieth birthday with surprise. Everything in between was a blur of work, bills, and doctors—endless, endless streams of doctors.

"...floaters. Quite common after surgery, especially in patients of your age."

"Huh?"

I'd not been paying attention. I was sure the doctor thought I had some kind of early-onset dementia, even though he smiled kindly and repeated himself. He wasn't any younger than me. Still, sitting in this reclining chair in the tiny room, I felt ancient.

"So these floaters will go away? I'm not going to spend the rest of my life seeing shadows creeping around?"

It was irritating. In a way, it was more irritating than the cataracts had been. Every time I tried to focus on the shadows, they flitted out of sight. Sometimes they remained, moving to stay at the corner of my vision as if they were trying to get my attention but didn't want me to look directly at them.

"Individuals prone to cataracts are sometimes prone to floaters, so while the condition might resolve somewhat as your eyes continue to heal, you may continue to have them. Eventually, you'll get used to the dark spots and will no longer notice them."

"They're not spots," I argued. Doctors didn't intimidate me as they used to, and I'd found that it was important to properly articulate symptoms. "They're elongated, with protuberances. They look like human shadows, only there's no one casting them."

Doctor Berkowitz patted me on the back of my hand. I wondered if I'd be offered a lollypop upon completion of the appointment. Or perhaps a bottle of prune juice.

"Well, the floaters *can* take on an oblong shape."

I was subjected to a long monologue about vitreous fluid, then urged to contact him immediately if I began seeing flashes of light, or the floaters appeared as groups. Lovely. Basically, they might resolve over time, or they might not. I'd traded horrible night vision and fading eyesight for floaters, and I'd paid over six thousand dollars for the privilege.

Six thousand dollars I could scant afford. I still caught my breath thinking about it, but after spending over ten years neglecting my own health, I'd needed to do this. I'd been given this new chapter in the autumn of my life. It was like breaking the water's surface for a gasp of air after nearly drowning. My eyesight had been my reward for survival.

"...avoid bright light. Wear sunglasses when you go out, and limit computer usage."

Nope. I mean, I was fine with the sunglasses thing, but there was no way I giving up my internet. Funny cat videos had become a highlight of my evenings.

And how sad was that? I was sixty, not ninety. Sheesh.

I left the genial Dr. Berkowitz, eyes properly shielded from the noon sunlight by my spanking new drug store sunglasses. A shadow moved from the corner of the building, falling in behind me off to the right. I sighed in resignation, mentally welcoming the new addition to my life. At least I could read, drive at night, and knit. Actually, I couldn't knit. I should really take up knitting. That seemed to be an appropriate activity for a woman my age. I envisioned myself rocking on my front porch, brightly colored yarn spilling from my lap as two needles clacked away. That would be fun. I could make scarves to give the neighbors for Christmas, and perhaps knit socks to send the troops overseas, or baby hats for the hospital. Yeah. Knitting.

"Come on, Mr. Floater. We've got to run to MegaMart, then meet our potential new roomie at four. After that we've got boxes in the attic to go through. If you're good, maybe I'll let you pick the movie tonight."

CHAPTER 3

J got a seven-layer bean dip, some pastries for breakfast, and a stash of toilet paper that would probably last me through the apocalypse. With a potential roommate moving in, one had to be prepared for anything. I also picked up the cat food, which had been my original purpose for coming to the gigantic discount store, along with a jumbo-sized box of litter, and some intriguing catnip-stuffed toys.

Taco—yes, my cat's name was Taco—deserved some toys. I'd never had a pet before, but on my way home from the cemetery the day of the funeral, I'd found myself terrified to return to an empty house. I'd detoured to the local animal shelter, arriving an hour before closing to stare at the furry occupants of wire cages, all waiting for new homes. After spending the last decade taking care of Eli, I decided that a dog would be too much for me. I didn't want something that needed regular walks or an excessive amount of attention. I wanted something that made the house feel less lonely, that would just meander around. Something that would require a minimal amount of care.

So I chose the most aloof cat at the shelter—a gray tabby who stared at me with dispassionate green eyes. The shelter employees had been thrilled. It seemed that spring was kitten season, and they were nearing capacity, which meant the less friendly and affectionate cats might find themselves on a cold metal table with a needle in their leg. It made me feel even more noble for giving this reserved cat a home.

When the paperwork was being filled out, they asked me his name. In spite of my journalist background, I wasn't the most creative woman in the world. I'd looked out the window in desperation and my eyes had lit on a sign for a nearby fast-food chain. Thus, my new pet was named Taco.

Once home, Taco revealed that his performance at the shelter had been an act and that he was a cat worthy of an Academy Award. My standoffish feline suddenly wanted on my lap every time I sat down. He was constantly weaving around between my legs, jumping on my kitchen counters, sleeping at the end of my bed, patting me awake in the morning with soft paws on my face.

Okay, I loved it. I never thought I would, but within the first twenty-four hours, this darned cat had become my lifeline. I hoped Judge Beck liked cats.

I was just heading to the checkout line when I saw clearance tables with stacks and stacks of books. It was a routine for me to cruise up and down these aisles, buying cookbooks that I'd never use, picking up forty-percent off biographies and the occasional evening read. Eli had always teased me about my romance novels until he realized that he got a heck of a lot more nookie when I was reading them.

Today there was an interesting do-it-yourself book on garden mosaics that I couldn't resist putting in my basket, and then at the end of the aisle a series of craft books—including a Learn To Knit kit which had knitting needles and a giant ball of colorful yarn.

I looked around as if I expected one of my neighbors to be spying on me and scrutinizing my purchases, then I threw the knitting kit into my cart, sliding it under the cat toys. I was sixty. I was a widow. I'd had cataracts. I'd just adopted a cat. Knitting seemed the next logical step to take in my new life. Plus, I was really interested in making those baby hats for the hospital.

Shopping done, I looped around the rear of the store, heading for the back strip where I'd parked my little Subaru. It wasn't that I was worried about someone scratching or dinging my fifteen-year-old car that had me parking way out in the sticks, it was my determination to get a little walk in my shopping expedition. In the last ten years, the walk to and from the store had sometimes been my only real bit of fresh air. Now it was just habit. Besides, I always felt like I should leave the closer spaces free for those who were in a hurry or who were struggling with baby strollers.

My cart squeaked as I rolled it over the blacktop past all the other cars and trucks. I nodded at a woman loading several industrial-sized boxes of diapers into her SUV, at a man carrying a forty-pack of festive Easter-themed cupcakes. Once past the other vehicles, nothing caught my eye beyond the familiar shadow that seemed to be following me nearly every day.

"Get lost, Mr. Floater. I'm hoping to see a different spirit, or maybe none at all. Leave me alone."

With a movement that looked suspiciously like a bow, my shadow disappeared, leaving me with clear eyesight and amazing peripheral vision. I stopped the cart in the middle of the aisle and waited, feeling foolish and wondering if maybe this was all in my head. Perhaps Doctor Berkowitz had been right and the shadows were only a side effect of my surgery.

Nothing. Just the very back of a parking lot with my Subaru surrounded by acres of empty spaces. Past the parking area was a steep weed-covered hill, then the guardrail and busy street. To my left was an expanse of prickly brush and more weeds leading down to a drainage pond, then up to the interstate. Across the interstate, the truck stop sign blinked. I'd been here thousands of times, parked at the very back of this lot more than I could remember, seen the same surroundings each time I frequented this store, but today was different. Today, something about this place gave me a chill, like it was waiting, dreading, anticipating, like the very air was strung tight as a wire about to break.

I shivered, then continued on to my car, the cart sounding louder than it should on the rough pavement. I wanted to get out of here. I wanted to go home. And inexplicably, I didn't want to ever come back.

CHAPTER 4

I was having wine at three o'clock in the afternoon on the front porch with my friend and neighbor, Daisy. Pinot Grigio, to be precise. Daisy was the sort of friend who often proclaimed that it was five o'clock somewhere, so she was heartily supportive of my early booze binge. Taco had been keeping us company, meowing and circling around our ankles until he realized our wine-fest didn't include any crackers or cheese that he could beg from us. I eyed his round form as he bounded from my porch into the bed of hostas, only his gray tail visible, flickering back and forth among the big green leaves. He was getting fat. I really should look into diet cat food, or maybe stop giving him treats from my own meals. It was hard to resist his earnest pleas for food, though. I was beginning to believe that cats had mind-control abilities. *Must give cat some of my baked chicken. Must give cat more baked chicken.*

"Are we celebrating or drowning our sorrows?" Daisy asked, pouring a generous amount into my extra-large sized wine goblets. I knew what she meant. Lately, there had been more of the sorrow drowning and a lot less of the celebrating. She was a good friend, always there to let me cry on her shoulder and to refill my glass when the reality of Eli's death hit me hard, or when I was staring down a stack of bills.

"I'm not sure," I told her honestly. It seemed a little premature to celebrate my being able to keep the house. For all I knew Judge Beck wouldn't show, or would hate it, or I would hate him. "I guess I can celebrate my ophthalmologist appointment today. It seems the cataract surgery was a success and I'm good to go."

I didn't tell her about the floaters. Although maybe they weren't floaters at all. Did grief and financial stress cause people to hallucinate? I was beginning to wonder.

Daisy lifted her glass in a toast and downed a hearty mouthful of wine. We were an odd pair to have developed such a close friendship. She was five years younger than me, with a platinum blonde curly hairdo that, judging by her roots, was a far cry from the salt-and-pepper nature had delivered. She was lean, athletic, and tan. She taught yoga at the Y, and had a social schedule that a celebrity would envy. She'd never been married, never had children, and under her cheerful, sassy exterior was a hurt I'd never been able to uncover.

"How's Reality-Show Pierson?" she asked.

J.T. Pierson was my boss, the man who'd been kind enough to hire a former journalist with a big blank of ten years on her resume. I was grateful, and I actually enjoyed the work.

"No major television studio has come calling. I think he's considering starting his own cable access channel, or possibly a YouTube videocast if he doesn't land a big contract soon."

Daisy sniffed, taking another sip of the wine. "Isn't there some client confidentiality or something where he can't broadcast that stuff? Is he going to change names to protect the not-so-innocent?"

I shrugged. "No idea. It's all public record, so I'd assume not. That bounty hunter guy does it on his reality show, and they name names in true crime fiction. I'm not lawyer, but I assume it's all above board."

With J.T. Pierson, one never knew, although I felt a bit guilty thinking such bad thoughts about the man who'd hired me when it seemed no one else would. He was kind, but he did walk the edge of what might be considered ethical behavior. I'd been a journalist for almost thirty years. I'd skirted those edges before, even though I liked to consider myself a fairly moral person. When it came to finding out the truth, or delivering justice, sometimes one needed to put a toe into dangerous waters.

I was sure I'd be toeing those waters regularly in my current job, too. As of last week, I was employed to do skip-tracing for Pierson Investigative and Recovery Services. I found people and turned them over to the authorities and/or their creditors to be held accountable for debt or other legal matters. I loved the research, and J.T. kept me busy with an endless stream of bad-debt and bounced-check traces while he handled the bail-jumpers. That meant he worked with the police while I sat in front of a computer all day. It was an ideal work arrangement.

"Hey." Daisy had a gleam in her blue eyes as she sat the wine glass down and leaned forward. "Think Pierson knows anything about the sex scandal? I'm dying to know who Caryn Swanson's girls were. I'm betting that Suzette Garnet is one. And I can't wait to find out who's in that black book."

Everyone wanted to know the answers to these questions. Especially Daisy who loved being in-the-know in our small town. "She's using us for bail, but I don't get involved in that side of the business. J.T. did say that Madam Caryn claims she doesn't keep client lists. According to her, she is a go-between for a fee. The girls keep their own lists, if they choose. And she's refusing to identify her 'girls'."

I knew this because J.T. was just as much of a gossip as Daisy.

My friend snorted. "Right. What kind of Madam doesn't keep a list, especially when she can use it in a plea bargain? I wonder if she'll turn over any of her 'girls' once she realizes she's facing jail time?"

I gulped my wine, wondering if I was going to become one of those old ladies who gossiped about the neighbors all the time, thinking that every young, attractive woman in stilettos, like Suzette Garnet, was a prostitute. Next thing I knew, I'd be shouting at people to get off my lawn and harassing the newsboy.

I was mid-swallow, glass still lifted when I saw the man climbing the wide wooden steps to my porch. It was four and this was my potential roommate. Nathanial Beck looked fortyish, too young to be a judge, but Locust Point was a small town and Milford, the county seat, wasn't huge compared to larger cities. His was an appointed position, and it was completely reasonable to assume a lawyer with a solid career and reputation could find himself a small-county judge at forty.

Or he was older, and just looked good. He did look good with blond, sun-streaked hair and darker eyebrows in a tanned face. Those eyebrows practically hit the roof when he saw us...saw me.

Sweet mother of a biscuit. Here was a judge, my potential boarder, arriving to find me and Daisy Mercer boozing it up on my front porch. So much for being an upstanding land-lord who could show steady and decent character in his custody case.

I scooted the glass of wine aside and stood, shaking his

hand. He had a firm handshake, his wrist ornamented with a heavy, expensive watch. It wasn't like the diamond-studded Rolex that J.T. flashed around. This watch looked like you could drag it fifty leagues under the sea and it would still keep amazingly accurate time.

"I'm Kay Carrera." I gestured to my companion, who, instead of standing and greeting my guest, stared open-mouthed, a raised glass of Pinot Grigio in her hand. "This is my friend and neighbor, Daisy Mercer."

"I'm Nathanial Beck. Carson told me that you were considering taking in renters. If this is a bad time…" His voice trailed off. His gaze shifted to Daisy, then to the bottle of wine—the nearly empty bottle of wine.

I heard Daisy's teeth click as she shut her mouth, then the clink of her wine glass on the table. "Oh, no. I was just leaving. We were celebrating…. celebrating something."

Great. *Thanks a lot, Daisy.*

"I just had cataract surgery and the doctor gave me the all clear this morning." I smiled up at him. "I haven't had much cause to celebrate lately." My smile wobbled.

His hazel eyes widened. I saw something in his expression besides sympathy, something that I thought might be a hint of wistfulness. "Of course. I'm so sorry for your loss, Mrs. Carrera. Please accept my condolences on the passing of your husband."

I felt guilty, like I was using the death of my spouse to turn his view of me from boozing lush to one of a sad widow trying to find a moment of celebration in a sea of grief. But my words were true. I hadn't celebrated much of anything in the last decade, and although Daisy was always happy to come over and help me drown my sorrows in a bottle of wine, for the last few years these parties-on-the-porch had been a rare occurrence.

The grief came crushing back like the planet's gravity had

increased a hundredfold. My eyes burned with tears at his words of condolence, at the thought of all I'd lost. Eli hadn't been gone a month and I was still so very raw inside.

Daisy clattered in her high heels down the porch steps, promising to call me later. I blinked away the tears and gestured to the front door. "Please. Come in and let me show you around."

The front door was actually front doors—as in plural. They were narrow, oak, with little brass knobs and old-fashioned keyholes. Anyone wider than a broomstick had to open both of them or risk banging hips and shoulders against the jamb. They were an absolute pain when you were carrying groceries or a duffle bag—or when you were a six foot one judge with the shoulders of an Olympic swimmer.

"Charming," he commented as he wedged himself sideways through the opening.

They were, which was why Eli and I had left them instead of replacing them with a modern, normal-width doorway. I walked ahead, through what had originally been a formal parlor and was now much less formal sitting area. Built-in bookshelves were packed with fiction and nonfiction. Two recliners flanked a marble-topped table. The bow window had a pillow-filled seat with additional bookshelves underneath. Judge Beck nodded, his face expressionless. I waited a moment, then led him into the corner room that Eli and I had turned into our television area. I still got no reaction from the judge, so I proceeded to guide him into the dining room with my Aunt Hazel's giant mahogany table and chairs. Unable to take the silence, I started to babble about the original leaded glass windows and shutters. When Eli and I had bought the house, several of the windows had been replaced with modern, energy efficient ones. We'd spent many nights searching internet listings and getting quotes from contractors before we decided to take the plunge and rip out the modern windows, replacing them with antique ones that we found mostly at auctions and estate sales.

It had been a labor of love haunting the auctions up and down the coast, sometimes having to ship big heavy windows across several states, but when I looked out through the wavy glass to a bright and slightly distorted view, I felt like I was looking backward through the lens of time. Yes, my heating and air-conditioning costs were obscene, but it had been worth it.

"The kitchen has all modern appliances. We had the entire house rewired when we purchased it, and much of the plumbing is updated. The stereo in the TV room pipes music throughout the lower floor and even outside to the porch and the gazebo out back."

He nodded again. I was beginning to sweat at this point, worried that he hated it. How could he hate my beautiful home? It would be like hating a part of me.

"The house is three stories," I told him, retracing our steps to the front of the hallway to ascend the wide staircase. I ran my hand along the thick carved wood banister, reassured by the feel of the smooth, time-worn oak. "The top floor has two smaller bedrooms and a sitting area, while the second floor has four bedrooms including the master suite. The master is the only room with an in-suite bathroom, but there is a full bath at the end of the hall on each floor."

I showed him the three bedrooms on the second floor, deciding that he really didn't want to see the master suite where I was staying—where Eli and I had stayed until the accident after which the TV room had housed a giant bed with controls and side rails; a bed that adjusted with a tap of a button. I hated having it in there. I hated the ugliness of it in my home. I hated that I couldn't manage to get Eli up and down the stairs by myself. I hated everything it stood for— the sudden loss of my beloved husband to this invalid, this man I felt I didn't know. I hated it, but when they had come to take it away, I'd wept.

We had decorated and furnished all six bedrooms, even after we'd discovered that children weren't in our future. The bedrooms had come in handy for visitors or when friends wanted to stay after a particularly indulgent party. They weren't huge by modern standards, but I hoped the judge would find them acceptable.

"The third floor tends to be a bit hot in the summer," I confessed. "The rooms are smaller, and access is through a narrow back staircase. Originally it was where the servants lived. You're welcome to your pick of any rooms except the master suite, but if you're going to use the third floor bedrooms, you'll probably have to use the twin beds that are up there unless you can hoist them up to the top back porch and through the door there."

I was babbling again. If he turned it down, somehow it would be a reflection on me personally. I'd been originally conflicted about whether I wanted a roommate or not, but now I found myself desperately trying to convince him of the charm of my home.

"Can we redecorate?"

Hope bloomed somewhere in my chest. "Cosmetic stuff, yes. Paint. New area rugs. You can switch out the furniture if you want to use your own."

"I don't have any," he confessed, his tone just as expressionless as his face. "And honestly I was dreading having to go shopping for beds and dressers and all that. I was thinking more along the lines of paint, pictures—that sort of thing. Henry won't care as long as he can set up a television and an Xbox, but Madison will want to make her room into a teenage-girl paradise."

His lips twitched as he said the last bit, the stone-set of his eyes softening. Fathers and their daughters. I might not have kids of my own, but I could relate to this sort of relationship. My dad and I had been very close. So had mom and I, but in a different way. I'd read somewhere that girls use their father as a sort of template when dating. I didn't know how true that was. Eli had been very different on the surface than my policeman father, but deep down they had shared the same calm, unflappable demeanor, the same love of logic and procedure. And they both had hated paperwork with a passion.

"That won't be a problem," I told him.

The judge stood quietly for a few moments. That was when I decided I needed to break out the big guns and show him the part of the house where I had rarely ventured in the last decade.

"Come with me." I led him down the stairs, through the dining area and kitchen and down the narrow back servants' staircase. When I flicked on the lights, his jaw dropped. I couldn't help but smirk. Back then, when we'd remodeled the basement, the world had been our oyster, and Eli had spared no expense. The home theater set-up might be a bit dated, but it still wowed. No doubt his kids would have a blast tearing up the felt on the nine-foot pool table I'd given my husband for Christmas the year we'd finished renovations. And as for the wine cellar and the humidor—well, I'd keep those doors locked. It wasn't like there was much in there anymore. After the accident, expensive wine was no longer in my budget, and neither were Eli's pricey cigars.

"This... wow. The kids would love it here. They could each have their own room, and I wouldn't worry about them bothering you with their television shows if they came down here."

"The back yard is a good size, too. There's a hot tub and a gazebo, and a gas grill."

Eli and I used to entertain weekly. We'd barbeque and

hold informal wine tastings. We'd turn on the speakers and relax with our guests, chatting and reclining on the benches or admiring the herb garden I'd put in. The garden was now full of weeds. The hot tub sat empty. I couldn't recall the last time I'd started up the grill. For all I knew, it was full of wasps. But that would change. This was a good thing. This was a great thing. This house was too big for just me and a cat.

"Oh, I have a cat. I almost forgot to tell you. Is that okay?"

His eyes gleamed with a wicked delight. "That's perfect. Heather's allergic to cats, so we never had one. The kids will be thrilled."

I wasn't sure how I felt about Taco being the instrument of some passive-aggressive revenge between Judge Beck and his soon-to-be ex-wife, but I'd cope. I relaxed, feeling the financial pressures ease with his enthusiasm. "The kids are welcome to bring any game system they want and hook it up down here. I don't watch much television, and when I do, I tend to use the upstairs one, so they'd pretty much have free rein."

Judge Beck walked around the room, running a hand over teak trim on the pool table, and examining the dart board against the far wall. "I'd set rules. You wouldn't have to worry about the kids damaging anything."

Damage could always be repaired. This house needed some love. And this particular room had been neglected for too long. Honestly, it wasn't my lack of interest in television that had kept me from this section of the house. This had always been Eli's sanctuary, and after the accident, it had been too painful to be here, down steps he could no longer traverse. It had been one more thing the accident had stolen from him—from us.

"What's this room?"

My chest ached and I struggled to take a breath. "It's a

humidor. My husband went through a cigar phase, and this was a temperature and humidity-controlled room to store them." I swallowed the lump in my throat. "You don't need to worry about tobacco. I don't smoke, and there aren't many cigars in there anymore. The door next to it is a cellar for wine storage. There are locks on both doors."

My breath came back, too fast and hard. Once again, everything blurred before my eyes. I'd sold all the valuable cigars. I'd sold Eli's cigars. I didn't smoke, and after the accident, he couldn't, either. We'd needed the money, but oh…I'd give anything for him to be here blowing a puff of that nasty smoke in my face, chuckling as I complained.

He'd never known they were gone, never asked about them. Darn it all, he would have *wanted* me to sell them. Still, the memory rubbed a raw spot in my soul. I hadn't hurt this bad when I was packing up his clothing.

"It's okay." The judge's voice was soft, and I suddenly liked him—not just the fact that he was saving me from foreclosure, but *him*. "I'm glad you don't smoke, and wine behind a locked door isn't a problem."

I turned around, embarrassed that he'd seen me so vulnerable. "So… what do you think?"

The judge let out a long breath and walked around to face me as if he were about to confess something heinous.

"I don't know if Carson told you, but I'm going through a divorce and I'm trying for joint physical custody. Heather is fighting it with everything she's got. One of the keys to me getting joint custody is securing safe housing and maintaining a spotless reputation. Your house is the perfect environment. I'd love to rent three rooms and I'd be happy to sign a lease for two years. That's probably how long it will take for this divorce to be resolved."

And after that, he'd probably go buy a McMansion in the suburbs. It would give me a two-year reprieve to decide what

I wanted to do with the house. I was under no illusion that I could keep it long-term with my salary, but two years right now sounded like an eternity.

"Mrs. Carrera? Is that acceptable?"

"Kay." Out of his whole speech, I don't know why that stuck in my mind, but I didn't want my roommate to call me Mrs. Carrera. It made me feel like I was his old grade school teacher or like I was two steps from the nursing home. "Call me Kay."

He smiled. The smile was far too wide for him to be considered conventionally attractive, but something about it made me smile back. He seemed like a nice man. Reserved, law-abiding, trustworthy—an earnest and steady sort of man. "Kay, then. What are you asking for rent, Kay?"

I noticed that he didn't ask me to call him Nathanial, or Nate. It was just as well. He seemed so formal, that I honestly could only think of him as Judge Beck. I hoped I never got a traffic ticket and needed to appear in court before him. It would be so embarrassing.

I quoted a price, and, to his credit, the judge didn't flinch. He probably would be less flush than usual with a divorce in the works, but I had a mortgage to make. If I didn't get what I was asking, we'd all be out on the streets within a year.

"Deal."

I blinked. And just like that, I had a roommate—room-mates, actually, since the kids would probably be here often. I had roommates, and my mortgage would be covered every month for the next two years. It was like a crushing weight had been lifted from my shoulders.

"I'd like to move in tomorrow morning if possible."

That was terribly fast, but I guess things were awkward at home. Or maybe he was staying at a hotel. Either way, it wouldn't be a problem. "I'll give you a key. I don't have a lease ready, but I'll pull one together and have it for you when you arrive tomorrow."

I'd be spending a few hours cobbling one together from the internet, but that wasn't a problem, either. It wasn't like I had anything else on my agenda for tonight beyond watching cat videos.

"One more thing." The judge winced. "Heather will want to see the house, to meet you before I can have the kids here. I'd like her to come by tomorrow if it's okay. I'm sorry—I hate to dump you in the middle of such a tension-filled situation, but I need to play nice with her if I'm to have any chance at custody."

I was going to have to make polite conversation with a hostile wife. Thankfully, I didn't look like the type to be seducing her estranged husband or running naked through the house with the kids around—or *without* them around.

"That's fine. I'll be here."

He shook my hand. "Then I'll see you tomorrow, Kay."

Then he pulled out a checkbook. And just like that, half of the problems weighing down my mind vanished.

CHAPTER 5

he next day when Judge Beck showed up bright and early, I wasn't drinking wine on the front porch with Daisy. I was knitting. Well, I was *trying* to knit. I liked to think of myself as a determined, stick-with-it kind of woman, but my inability to connect loops together to form a useful and attractive object was disheartening. At least the cookies had turned out.

I'd always loved to bake. Non-baking foods were not always a success. My chicken sometimes had the texture and moisture of jerky. Rice stuck to the bottom of the pan. Noodles were limp and slimy, and steaks either we're-lions-in-the-Savannah rare or burnt to charcoal. But give me flour, butter, sugar, and eggs, and I could turn anyone into a type-two diabetic in seconds. Of course, I hadn't baked much of anything in the last ten years. Afraid that my skills had gone the way of my herb garden, I'd run to the grocery store last night and grabbed a giant tub of pre-made cookie dough. And then I'd come home to put on a kettle for tea and watch television reruns with Mr. Floater standing just off to the side. I was beginning to regret this cataract surgery. Being

LIBBY HOWARD

able to drive and read, and to see clearly was a miracle of modern medicine, but I wasn't sure the trade-off of visual hallucination was worth it.

Then I'd gone to bed and stared at the ceiling, wondering what my life was going to be like without Eli. I had work, but what about evenings and weekends? There was only so much television and cat videos I could watch, only so much wine-drinking on the porch with Daisy I could do, only so many cookies I could bake and eat. Even if I did manage to become reasonably proficient at this knitting thing, I couldn't spend every spare moment at it. What did I used to do before I married Eli? Hike? Ride a bike? Go to concerts? Would it be weird for a sixty-year-old woman to go to a concert? Maybe I should look into taking a college class in the evenings.

I'd tossed and turned so much that Taco had abandoned me for his kitty bed by the dresser. After finally falling asleep around two in the morning, I got up at six to bake cookies and learn to knit. The cookies had turned out perfect, as store-bought ready-made dough always does. Taco got to taste-test one for quality assurance and gave it his approval before heading outside for his morning activities. I ate a few with my coffee, then just to make sure everything today went off without a hitch, I lit a sugar-cookie scented candle. The house smelled like a bakery, and the cut-glass serving platter in the living room loaded with peanut butter cookies completed the illusion.

If only my knitting was going as well. It had taken me a half an hour just to decipher the instructions for casting-on. The knit part seemed to be okay, but no matter how many times I read the directions for the purl stitch, it ended up looking just like the knit one. I'd ripped it out three times and gotten out a magnifying glass to look at the step-by-step illustrations, just in case there was something I was missing. By the time Judge Beck arrived, I had a seven-by-two-inch rectangle of loopy mess. I was never so grateful to see someone in my life. I tossed the horrible example of my handiwork next to the tray of cookies on the living room table, and offered to help him carry boxes upstairs.

He looked appalled, as if I'd just offered to change his car tire or bench-press a refrigerator.

"No, no. I've got it. You—" He abruptly stopped at the foot of the stairs and sniffed.

"Have a cookie," I offered. Then I realized he could hardly take a cookie when his hands were occupied with the large box, so I did what any eccentric woman who'd been taking care of a disabled husband for ten years would do. I picked up a cookie and shoved it in his mouth.

Judge Beck was tall. He was also carrying a big box. So I had to reach up and around the box to cram the crumbly peanut butter treat into his mouth. He blinked in surprise, mumbled something, then walked up the stairs while chewing.

I surveyed the foyer/living room area. Cookies. Knitting. Taco snoozing at the edge of the window seat, paw twitching as he dreamed. Boxes in the corner of the room ready for the charity to pick up. It wasn't perfect, but it would have to do. The only thing I needed was a carafe of fresh coffee and I'd be ready for my new housemates.

I had just filled the carafe when I heard voices at the door. A deaf person could have heard them, as loud as they argued.

"I'm not letting the children stay overnight here. I'm not even letting them out of the car until I see that this is a suitable environment."

"Knock it off, Heather. You nixed the idea of me renting an apartment saying there wasn't enough space for the kids. Until the divorce is final, I can't access savings to buy anything. It's either this or an apartment. Take your pick."

"I'm not having my kids exposed to some floozy. If you

want even minimal visitation, you've got to let me approve where they'll be staying and who they'll be living with."

"Oh, like I had any say-so about you introducing them to Tyler. I've got no idea if he's spending the night, sleeping in *our* home, in *our* bed while our children are one thin wall away. She's a widow, Heather. And she's at least twenty years my senior."

What happened to the calm, unemotional man I'd seen yesterday? It seems divorce brought out the worst in everyone. This had to stop before Judge Beck's temper ruined everything and I found myself looking for cheap one-bedroom apartments once more. I practically ran from the kitchen, slowing to a sedate walk and composing a pleasant smile as I entered the foyer.

"It's so nice to meet you. I'm Kay Carrera. I was just in the kitchen getting some coffee together." I held up the carafe and put it near the cookies, scooting my horrible knitting aside to set a handful of mugs on the table. "Would you like some? Cream or sugar? Cookies? You must be Heather. Are the kids still in the car?"

I shook her hand, waving her farther into the house and nudging a surprised Judge Beck aside with my elbow. Outside, a shiny late model Cadillac Escalade was parked at the curb. The passenger door was open, and with a quick glance I saw a dark-haired girl typing on her cell phone.

Heather stared at me in shock, no doubt taking in my baggy jeans and bohemian smock as well as my mussed hair. I was far from the floozy she expected. It might sting a bit to hear myself described as the much-older widow, but I needed to get used to it. I was a widow, and in society's eyes, I was almost old enough to be Judge Beck's mother. It was time to embrace the new me.

Heather had finished giving me an incredulous once-over and begin taking in the room. I gestured toward the boxes, still stacked by the door. "Please excuse the mess. My husband passed away last month and I'm still going through his things. Those were supposed to be picked up yesterday, but the charity can't make it until Monday morning."

Her face turned red. On the pantone scale, it would have been about one-ninety-two. "Oh. I didn't realize... Nate said you were a widow, but I didn't know it had been so recent. I'm so sorry for your loss."

I couldn't dwell on that right now. I couldn't let myself start crying like I seemed to do every time someone offered their condolences. Yes, my heart hurt but I needed to look ahead to my future— a future that hopefully involved a roommate and his two teen children.

"Judge Beck told me you have two teenagers," I said. "It will be so lovely to have them here. Eli and I tried, but we were never blessed with children of our own."

"Yes... two children. I'm... yes, two children. Madison is in high school, and Henry is in junior high. Are you sure? I mean, they're teens, and if you're not used to children, you might find them too noisy or rambunctious."

I heard a snort from Judge Beck. "Trying to scare her off, Heather? Trying to make sure I'm back in a hotel room so you can push for full custody? That's low, even for you."

Oh no. Not this again. I needed to defuse this and fast. "The house has six bedrooms, so each of them can have their own room. There is a television and recreation room in the finished basement." I turned to face her, giving her my most yearning, I-love-teenagers expression. "A house like this longs to hear the laughter of children. I hope you'll allow yours to stay here. It would really mean a lot to me."

I knew I was laying it on a bit thick, but few things tugged at a woman's heartstrings like a childless, sixty-year-old widow in an enormous Victorian mansion. Besides, I *was* rather excited to have the kids here. I'd baked cookies. I'd stocked up on sodas and snack foods. I'd even bought an extra chicken to roast for dinner.

Heather blinked, her gaze shifting between her husband and me. "Um, I'd love a cup of coffee. Black, please. No sugar."

A woman after my own heart. Honestly, I didn't have anything against Heather Beck. I had no idea what had gone on between her and her husband and I didn't want to know. She hardly looked like the gold-digging baby-mama I'd envisioned. Instead of the bleach-blonde, plastic-surgery-enhanced woman in high heels that I'd expected, Heather seemed like a cross between a soccer mom and business-casual executive. Her long, dark brown hair was neatly secured at the nape of her neck. Her make-up was subtle and tastefully done. She had on olive-green pants and a scoop-neck t-shirt that didn't show the slightest bit of cleavage. Actually, I wasn't sure she had much cleavage to show. Her trim figure seemed more super-model thin than porn-star lush.

I fixed her a cup of coffee and again offered her a cookie, smiling as she took one.

"What are you making?" she asked, eyeing my knitting.

I had no idea. I thought it was supposed to be a wash-cloth, but my effort didn't look anything like the one in the picture. "I'm just learning, so it's for practice. I'm hoping to make hats for newborn babies at the hospital, and some socks to send to the soldiers."

She nodded, that stunned look still on her face. "You do a lot of charity work?"

No. I'd been too busy taking care of Eli the last ten years to even think of charity work. "I'd like to, now that I have some time on my hands. I'm mostly just trying to keep busy, but I'd like to start volunteering and doing more of this sort of thing."

"Of course." She glanced out to her open car door, a small frown creasing her brow, as if she were deciding whether or not to allow the kids across the threshold.

"Do you want to see the bedrooms?" I asked, praying with all my might that she liked my house and liked me. It would make things so much easier if she felt at ease around here, felt she could have a civil, even friendly, conversation with me. I'd never worked so hard in my life to win someone over.

Heather gave her car another anxious look and nodded. I showed her around, giving her pretty close to the same spiel that I'd given Judge Beck. As I showed her the back yard, our conversation shifted to trivial topics like which companies might sponsor a boat in the summer regatta and if the high school softball team had a chance at going to state. We made our way back to the front of the house via the wrap-around porch and she halted, eyeing the car once more.

"Come on kids," she finally called out. "Come see Daddy's new place and meet Mrs. Carrera."

"About time," the girl groused, swinging long legs out of the passenger seat and slamming the door with a swing of her hips. Madison got her height from her father, with her mother's dark hair and lean figure. She also had enough eye makeup on to make Alice Cooper jealous.

The back door opened and a boy hopped out. He was all legs and arms, a shock of light brown hair dipping over one eye. He shambled up to me, with his basketball shorts, over-sized tank top, and unlaced sneakers. Where Madison's eyes never left her phone, Henry's gaze was direct. He grinned.

"'Sup?"

My lips twitched in return. "The sky," I teased.

Madison rolled her eyes. The good news was that meant I could actually see her eyes, since she'd looked up from her phone at my comment. They were hazel, like her father's.

"Henry, Madison, this is Mrs. Carrera. I want you to be respectful of her house while you're here. Got that?"

Madison ignored her. Henry gave his mother a peace sign.

"I made cookies. They're just inside the door. And if you don't drink coffee, I have juice and milk in the fridge. And sodas. I've got lots of sodas."

That got them moving. Henry was off like a shot, nearly colliding with his father at the front door.

"Hey!" Judge Beck's face lit up and he caught the boy in a hug. Both kids erupted into a chorus of "Dad! Dad!" and I was thrilled to see Madison shed her sullen teenager persona and wrap her arms around her father. They were like one big pile of hugging affection. I smiled, my heart warm at the sight. Then I turned to Heather.

The woman stood still, a look of sorrow on her face. She took a deep breath, and as she let it out, her expression changed to one of stubborn determination. "I'll pick them up at five," she said. "Have them ready, please."

Judge Beck looked up, and the happy family spell was broken. Both kids scooted past him into the house to find the cookies, and Madison shoved her phone in the back pocket of her skinny jeans.

The judge's face hardened to match his wife's. "I will," he replied coolly, then turned his back on her to grab another box from the porch.

It was awkward to witness their animosity, their rudeness toward each other. I felt like I'd been caught snooping on their raw, private pain. Heather looked just as out of place as I felt. She fumbled with her keys, opening her mouth as if she wanted to say something, then shutting it with a shake of her head.

"Thank you, Mrs. Carrera. I enjoyed the tour. Your house is lovely."

"Kay. Call me Kay," I told her, not wanting her to leave under the weight of this tension.

She smiled back at me as she walked to the Escalade. It was a wobbly smile that tugged at my heartstrings. "Thanks, Kay. Please call me Heather."

I watched her drive off. The children were inside exclaiming over Taco. Judge Beck squeezed through the doorway with another box, reminding them to thank me for making the cookies. Things were changing quicker than I could manage. Eli was gone, and in his place was a judge twenty years my junior, his two teens, and my new pet cat.

I felt the tickle of fur against my leg, the rumble of purring, and reached down to scoop Taco into my arms. His fur was soft and warm, and he nuzzled against me with approval as I petted him. The stormy waters of my life would eventually still. This was my new normal now. A house full of people. A job across from the courthouse. And this furry guy who I wouldn't trade for the world.

"Come on, Taco. Let's see if there are any cookies left for us."

CHAPTER 6

*T*aco scampered in the door, giving the kids another chance to admire his magnificence while I stooped to pick up the newspaper from the smashed flower bed. I didn't know my paper delivery person. Unlike the oldies sitcoms of kids on bikes, my daily news was brought by a shadowy figure who launched it from a dark sedan in the wee hours of the morning. It was like a drive-by from a '40s gangster movie, except instead of bullet holes in my porch, I had crushed flowers. I thought about calling to complain, but I was worried there might be retaliation involving cement shoes or something.

Front page was, of course, news about the arrest of the madam. I blinked in surprise at the picture that accompanied the article. I didn't know Caryn Swanson personally. I wasn't like I needed her services as a wedding planner, and hadn't attended, let alone hosted, any swank parties in the last ten years requiring an event consultant. She didn't look anything like I'd imagined. When I thought of a woman running a house of prostitution—even if that "house" was meeting johns in hotel rooms—I thought of an older, former prostitute, someone who chain-smoked and wore clothing better suited to a woman half her age. Caryn Swanson was young— mid-twenties at the most. And she was very pretty. I squinted at the picture, wondering if they'd been able to get anything recent, and this was from twenty years ago. Because if this was what Caryn Swanson looked like now, she was probably able to earn a few bucks turning tricks herself. Although maybe she didn't do that sort of thing, instead taking a percentage off the top and keeping her own body out of the equation.

I stood at the doorstep and read the article. Still no black book, although rumors were running wild about whose names might be inside. As Daisy had said, Caryn was also still refusing to name the prostitutes that worked for her. The statement her lawyer had released to the press said she was completely innocent, and that this was a terrible mistake made by an overzealous officer.

A few "unnamed sources" said that Caryn Swanson conducted this side of her business through online ads, screening clients then organizing the times and locations for the meetups. She had a list of "service providers" and matched them according to a client's needs and prefer- ences. The reporter conjectured that her clients included those who requested extremely kinky stuff, thus her insis- tence on not revealing either her client list or her providers.

Or maybe she was innocent. Maybe she'd offered the undercover cop a threesome with a girlfriend and he'd misunderstood. Maybe Locust Point was so eager for juicy gossip that "unnamed sources" were coming out of the woodwork with bizarre, fabricated tales.

Was it wrong of me that I was one of those residents eagerly devouring the juicy gossip? Prostitutes in Locust Point and neighboring Milford. Kinky stuff. Mystery clients.

If that black book was ever found, whose names would be in it? My journalist/skip-tracer self was intrigued.

I folded the paper under my arm, vowing to do some research of my own later, and headed in. The hallway was empty. The cookie plate was empty beyond a few crumbs that Taco was busy consuming. I shooed him off the table and took the platter into the kitchen, beginning to feel a bit like a stranger in my own home. I could hear the footsteps as well as muffled voices from upstairs, and vowed to not make a pest of myself. I was curious, though—curious what Judge Beck was moving into his room besides clothing and toiletries, curious what the kids thought of their rooms, my house, the cookies… and me. But they were roommates, not family come to visit. I needed to allow them their private space and their time to be together. Alone. Without an unknown woman getting in the middle of their family business. So I turned on some background music to mask their presence, looked up a few recipes for coffee cakes, then sat down once again with my knitting.

Whoever said that knitting was a Zen, meditative exercise had probably never picked up a needle. The gigantic metal sticks felt awkward in my hands. The loops kept sliding off the end, unraveling a line of stitches vertically down the washcloth. I still couldn't figure out how to do the purl stitch. My soft, whispered words of frustration became a sort of mantra to be chanted as I worked. Finally, around lunchtime, I cast off the last row, surveying my handiwork.

It wasn't a sweater. It wasn't a baby hat. It was a simple washcloth. It was supposed to be an easy first attempt at what I'd hoped would be a rewarding and interesting hobby, but this thing on my lap had turned out to be a trapezoid-shaped mess that had lumpy rows and loopy stitches. It also had long strings hanging at either end from the cast on and cast off. I wasn't sure what to do with them. I had a bad premonition that if I trimmed them close, the end would slip through the knot and unravel the whole darned thing the moment I tried to wipe a dish. After working so diligently on it, I didn't want to wind up with a long string of yarn.

Finally, I decided to make six more knots in the end and slap a dot of glue on it, just to make sure the knots stayed put. Feeling rather pleased with myself, I took it to the kitchen and draped it over the sink faucet. Then I made lunch.

"Making" lunch consisted of opening a tub of store-bought chicken salad and scooping it into a pretty bowl. The same routine occurred with macaroni salad and chips. Struck by a spirit of hostess-ness, I even put the potato rolls in a cloth-lined basket, and squirted condiments into little glass bowls complete with tiny individual knives. Everything went on the dining room table. I made sure Taco was out of the house and not planning a sneak attack on the food the moment my back was turned, then I called up to let everyone know I had lunch on the table.

The stampede of elephant footsteps on the stairs let me know the kids weren't ones to ever be late to a meal, but when Judge Beck came down, the odd expression on his face had me questioning the whole thing. Was this too much? Maybe I should have just told them there was bologna in the fridge and gone out for the day? I didn't want to interfere with their move-in/family time, but the judge clearly hadn't had a chance to do any grocery shopping.

"You weren't going to take them out for lunch, were you?" I waved a hand at the table. "I ran back to the grocery store last night and picked up some food. I figured you all would be hungry."

"No. I mean I guess eventually we would have gotten something." He hesitated a moment and took a breath. "I appreciate all this, really I do. I just don't want you to think that you're obliged to feed us."

I understood the words behind the words. Roommates to him didn't mean room and board. Although I now felt embarrassed at my luncheon largess, I was a bit relieved. I remembered how much teenagers ate, and if the dent they were making in the chicken salad was any indication of their food consumption levels, rent wouldn't have covered both the mortgage and the grocery bill. But what to do with that extra chicken I'd bought for tonight? Freeze it? Or cook it up and make some actual homemade chicken salad next time?

No, there would be no next time. Into the freezer it would go.

"Only this once." I smiled at him. "You just moved in. You haven't had a chance to get groceries. And I'm sure you'd rather spend your afternoon going out to buy stuff for the kids' rooms instead of having to go get lunch."

"Well, thank you." His shoulders relaxed, and there was even a hint of a smile in return.

There was just enough chicken salad left for me to make myself a sandwich. After eating, the kids helped clean up with some prompting from their father, then they all piled out the door, only to return several hours later with enormous shopping bags full of decorative pillows, throw rugs, and posters. Judge Beck began hauling in groceries, and the rest of the day was more relaxed, with the kids trotting up and down the stairs, and the judge finding room in the refrigerator for his food.

Heather showed up at five to pick up the kids and was immediately dragged upstairs to see their rooms. The tension returned the moment her SUV pulled up to the curb. Judge Beck followed them around, like he was afraid Heather was going to steal the silver. She didn't look at him once. Neither spoke to one another.

"I'll bring them by next Friday after school." Heather told the wall beside Judge Beck's head once the kids were out the door and climbing into the Escalade. I noticed that once again Madison was nose-down into her phone, a frown creasing her forehead.

Judge Beck glared at his wife. "Monday night through Thursday morning this week. We agreed—"

"They have school," Heather argued to the wall. "If you're going to drop them off at my house at seven in the morning and pick them up at my house at six at night, then I might as well have them those days."

"I will pick them up and drop them off at school." The judge's tone was pretty close to the temperature of dry ice. "There's no need for them to go to and from your house. Those are my days this week."

Heather's mouth thinned into a tight line. "You have to be at court at eight, and your cases run until five. How are you—"

"That's my business, not yours," he snapped. "I'll make sure my caseload works around their school schedule on the days I have them."

"Nice that you can do that now. Where was all this flexibility when we were together, huh?"

I held my breath. Yes, I was eavesdropping. And neither one of them seemed to care that they had an audience.

Judge Beck gritted his teeth, then that cold, distant mask came over his face once again. "I haven't seen them for more than a few hours here and there in the last month. You agreed to this in mediation. I will pick up the kids from school on Monday and they will be with me until I drop them off at school on Thursday morning. End of discussion."

Heather's mouth twisted. She spun on her heel, still not looking directly at her husband, and then she left without another word. I watched her stomp down the walkway, fearing for her cute sandals. Madison looked up as her mother approached. Still frowning, she looked back down at her phone, sparing one of her typing hands to swing her door closed. I heard the slam of the driver's door, then the squeal of the SUV pulling away from the curb.

When I turned around, Judge Beck was gone.

* * *

I'D NEVER FELT SO AWKWARD in my own home. I threw the chicken in the oven to roast, hoping the smell might entice my new roommate to come down. After that I wandered around the first floor, read my newspaper, and tried once again to master the art of the knitted washcloth. I truly hoped to be able to one day make those baby hats I'd told Heather about, but at this rate, such an endeavor would likely be far in my future. After an hour of frustration, I tossed aside what was fast becoming another loopy rectangle and headed out to the back yard with a glass of iced tea to listen to the birds sing their sunset melodies and to enjoy the cool of the spring evening.

That was the moment when I truly realized what a mess my back yard had become. I remembered the parties that we had hosted with our friends, Eli at the grill, a spatula in one hand and a beer in the other. He'd joke about how his talent in surgery translated into a remarkable ability to cook burgers and hot dogs. Carson would tease him that he should be butchering the cow rather than cooking it. We'd drink juleps with fresh mint from my garden, and Kylie Minogue piped from the speakers.

The grill was rusted, unused for years. My herb garden was filled with weeds. The paint on the gazebo was peeling. I sat my tea on the porch step and knelt down into the damp ground, pulling grass and dandelions while the light grew dim around me. By the time I stood to head back in, the herb garden was a patch of bare dirt with a few sad, scraggly bits of green. I'd need to replant the basil, oregano, and dill, but the mint and lavender had somehow managed to survive under all those weeds. Tough plants, hunkering down and lasting through the years of hardship. Kind of like me. Maybe with some weeding and pruning, I'd bounce back, too.

Taco rubbed against my legs, then went to explore the treasures I'd just revealed. Rolling in the weeds and chewing on a stem of mint, the cat looked up at me with his bright green eyes. I picked him up, relishing the feel of his warm, soft fur, the vibration of his purring as I cuddled him.

Oh, no, the chicken. Pushing an indignant Taco aside, I ran for the kitchen and threw open the oven door. It wasn't too bad. A little dry, which seemed to be the way my chicken always turned out. Trying in vain to distract Taco with some fresh cat food in his bowl, I set about preparing my evening meal.

I ate alone. Had the judge even come downstairs for a snack or had he stayed in his room the entire evening? I had mixed feelings about his absence. Part of me enjoyed having the house to myself one more time, unsullied by the presence of strangers. Part of me was well aware that he was upstairs and felt as if I were the worst hostess in all of history, that my renter didn't feel welcome enough to come downstairs even with the enticing aroma of slightly overcooked chicken in the air.

Later that night, after all the dishes were in the dishwasher, and the roasting pan was drying on the counter, I went downstairs. The bulb at the top of the staircase had blown, leaving me with a dark walk down one flight until I turned the landing and the lower one lit my way. It was cooler compared to the spring evening air that filtered through the upstairs windows. As my foot hit the landing, I walked through a cold spot that would have done a freezer proud. Weird. I'd need to check the heat vents and make sure they were fully open. Another item to add to my growing to-do list.

At the bottom step, I turned on the light, admiring the room. I'd always loved it down here. When we first bought the house, Eli had laughed at how much time I'd spent remodeling the cellar into this modern retreat. *Bat woman*, he'd teasingly called me, and from the damp chill and musty odor that had taken over, he would have been right. All it needed was a ceiling full of furry, winged creatures.

I flicked some dust from the edge of the pool table and frowned, disgusted with myself for neglecting this section of the house. Even after years of physical therapy had restored limited mobility, Eli had still been unable to negotiate stairs. He'd lived the last ten years of his life mostly in the first floor of the house, occasionally going outside to the garden when someone came over to help me get him in and out of his chair and through the narrow doors. It had seemed wrong to be down here without him, like I was abandoning him upstairs.

The golden glow from the track lighting illuminated the soft, wine-colored carpet and caramel leather sofas. The memories came back—of Eli and I curled up together watching a movie, the hand-crocheted afghan from his mother keeping the basement chill from our legs. We'd added special heaters when we put in the wine room and humidor. I flicked them on, turning up the temperature. Taco bolted down the stairs, leaping onto the back of a sofa and looking around as if he had seen something suspicious.

"Guard cat?" I teased him. "Or maybe you want to pick out the movie?"

The tabby made a weird squawking noise, his tail

swishing angrily around as his eyes fixed on the edge of the sofa.

"Oh, no you don't." I moved the old afghan away from the cat's sharp claws and knelt down in front of the DVDs stored in a rack under the wall-mounted television. "Action? Romance? Comedy?"

With a thump, the cat jumped from the sofa to the floor, strolling over and purring as he serpentined around my arms. "Comedy it is," I announced as I stood and slid *Young Frankenstein* into the player. Grabbing a bottle of wine from the depleted walk-in, I wiped the dust out of a glass with the bottom of my shirt and popped the cork. Eli would have had a fit over this dusty glass. Of course, Eli would have been firing up a cigar in spite of my complaints. I hadn't really minded the cigars. It was a ritual of ours—I disrespected the wine and didn't understand the pleasure of fine tobacco while he was woefully rustic in his movie tastes and couldn't tell a peony from a petunia. We'd exchange some teasing insults, then we'd curl up under the afghan, sip our wine, and watch whatever I'd chosen for the evening. Often his hands would wander. Some evenings we'd wind up doing far more under that afghan than cuddling. I always wondered if his mother would have been scandalized or have approved of our use of the wedding gift she'd labored over for months.

She probably would have approved. My mother-in-law always said one of the happiest days of her life had been our wedding—her only child and the woman who'd become like a daughter to her. She'd died a few years before Eli's accident and I'd been grateful she hadn't lived to see him like that—either in the hospital when I feared he wouldn't survive, or after, when I found myself married to a very different man than the one I'd said vows to at the altar.

But now Eli was gone, joining his parents and mine in the arms of God. It was just me tonight under the afghan. Tears stung my eyes, blurring Gene Wilder and Madeline Kahn on the screen. He'd left me all alone. What was I going to do with my life now that he'd left me?

Eli, how could you abandon me like this? We'd promised through sickness and in health. I kept my end of the bargain only to have you leave. I need you. I don't think I can make it alone.

Taco took that moment to jump into my lap, a warm affectionate ball of fur. The floater returned, looking as if a shadow had sat down next to me on the sofa. My grief eased just a bit as I petted my cat and remembered there was another person just two floors up from me. Maybe I wasn't as alone as I thought.

CHAPTER 7

I was awake before the sun, when the sky was gray with just a hint of pink in the east. I'd always been an early riser, and ever since Daisy had discovered this fact, she'd been hauling yoga mats over and forcing me to contort myself until the sun appeared above the horizon.

In spite of tossing and turning all night, I was still dressed and ready with time to spare, setting up the coffee for automatic brew and throwing some blueberry scones in a towel-lined basket. Taco was yowling for his food before the tablespoons of grounds hit the coffee filter. Our first day together, he'd been perplexed at my early start but the cat quickly got with the program, realizing that rising before dawn meant breakfast before dawn.

"I'm hurrying," I scolded, finishing up with the coffee and grabbing the bag of Happy Cat out of the cabinet. By the time I'd gotten the bag open, Taco had batted his bowl across the floor, trying to convince me in cat-language that he was on the brink of death by starvation. In reality, the cat had filled out quite a bit since I'd brought him home from the shelter. I wasn't sure how fat was too fat when it came to cats. I wondered again if I should put Taco on a diet. Would he hate me forever if I gave him just a little less food in his bowl?

The eager way he shoved his head into the dish as I poured the Happy Cat did more for my sense of well-being than the hour of sunrise yoga. Happy Cat. They should have called it Happy Pet-Owner.

Daisy showed up promptly at five. By then, Taco was licking the last crumb from his bowl. I piped some 1930s jazz through the outdoor speakers, trying to be mindful that the neighbors as well as my new roomie were probably still sleeping. Then Taco and I joined my friend in the garden—me to greet the day with vinyasas; the cat to go stalk insects in the hedges.

Daisy did a light stretch, spreading out her mat and eyeing the house suspiciously. "Please tell me those kids didn't spend the night."

I rolled my eyes. "No. And if they did, I doubt they'd be up at this ridiculous hour of the morning."

"Good." She put herself in mountain pose. "I don't want teenagers looking at my saggy old-lady butt."

I noticed she didn't seem to care if Judge Beck saw her saggy old-lady butt. The thought had me glancing back at the windows, then checking out the reflection of my own rear end. *Was* it saggy? Should I do squats? At my age, was it even worth the bother? Honestly, everything looked kind of saggy, but the wavy, leaded glass windows probably made my shape look worse than it most likely was.

Full of denial about time's effects on my body, I closed my eyes and breathed deep. We went through the poses, and by the time we were rolling up the mats, I did feel better. I might be barely able to touch my toes, but something about the rhythmic breathing and smooth motion of the exercise calmed my anxious mind.

"I've got scones today," I told Daisy as we headed up toward the kitchen door. This was our routine. Yoga, a cup of coffee and whatever breakfast pastries I'd picked up at the store, then Daisy left and I went about my day. It had started as Sunday morning yoga—a way to get me outside and provide a much-needed break from a life that had begun to exclude anything not related to housekeeping or caretaking. Other friends had drifted away, but not Daisy. Years after Eli's accident, she was still bringing over fresh tomatoes, casseroles, and the weekly bottle of wine. Gratitude didn't begin to describe what I felt toward my best friend and neighbor. Daisy was the only reason I'd managed to keep my sanity the last ten years. She was the reason I'd not lost my individuality or my soul in the never- ending grind of responsibility, duty, and guilt.

Guilt. Because when the man you loved wasn't the same, when a skilled surgeon can no longer manage to cut his French toast, when I'd had those horrible self-pitying moments where I'd wondered what my life would have been like if he'd died in that hospital room, that was when the guilt filled you up like a water balloon about to burst. Daisy kept me from losing myself. I didn't know if she realized how much she meant to me, yoga and crystals and blessing bags and all.

Even now. Ever since Eli had died, she'd been coming over most mornings, turning our weekly yoga into nearly a daily event. It was surprising how quickly this became a routine, how quickly I'd grown to treasure our quiet time together. It was a great way to start the morning, giving me a feeling of togetherness, of peace that stayed with me all day. Me and my best friend.

Today the peace lasted until I crossed the threshold into my kitchen. Judge Beck stood at the coffee maker wearing a pair of plaid flannel pajama bottoms and a crisp t-shirt. It was incredibly obvious to me that he'd thrown the shirt on at the last moment and that in his own home, he probably would have been at the coffeemaker half-naked.

That thought had me jerking to an abrupt stop. Daisy ran into my back. "Hey!"

Judge Beck turned around at her exclamation, tugging at his shirt self-consciously. The aloof, distant look descended on his face. "Is this coffee up for grabs?"

My morning routine with Daisy just became a plus-one. "Of course. And so are the scones." I pulled a handful of mugs out of the cabinet.

Judge Beck poured himself a cup-o-joe and started to walk out, before hesitating to eye the scones.

"Stay," I told him. "We're not *that* sweaty."

"Speak for yourself," Daisy muttered, wiping her face with a damp paper towel. "Are these hot flashes ever going to end? I'm fifty-five, darn it. I should be done with this by now."

"Shirley's didn't stop until sixty-two, poor thing. Hang in there, girl." I put a scone on a plate and handed it to Judge Beck, noting his horrified expression at our topic of conversation. Too bad. If he was going to live here, he was going to occasionally hear about the woes of menopause.

Daisy made a pfft noise, dumping what seemed like a half gallon of milk into her coffee. "I hope it's all over soon. I've been planning my crone ceremony for the last decade. You'll have to come and help me burn the tampon effigy I made, Kay. Every month I pray to the goddess I don't have to deal with this ever again, but clearly she has other plans."

Judge Beck eyed the doorway, no doubt wondering how he could edge past Daisy and escape. After spending all evening tiptoeing around, wondering if he was coming down for dinner or to socialize, I suddenly felt like laying it all out on the table. Maybe it was the early morning yoga, maybe it was the fact that I held my first cup of coffee, untouched in my hand. This was my house, my life. I'm sure he'd gotten used to monthly events with his wife and daughter. He'd need to get used to hot flashes and talk of irregular menstrual cycles.

But tampon effigies? What the heck was Daisy up to now? I'd joined in on a few of my friend's circle thingies a few decades back, the only one there who was not buck naked. I'd gotten drunk on ceremonial wine during a Beltane celebration. I'd helped her smudge a grove with something that I was pretty sure wasn't just sage and prairie grass, but burning tampons?

Whatever. Count me in. If Daisy wanted me to get naked and burn tampons, I was going to be there to help. Although I intended on keeping my clothing on.

CHAPTER 8

I rolled in to work bright and early, an extra cup of coffee in hand and a scone tucked in a Ziploc bag in my purse, just in case I got busy and worked through lunch. I was a skip tracer, which really wasn't a far cry from my original career as a news reporter. Both jobs meant I needed to know how to research and document findings. Both jobs involved writing, taking dry facts and presenting them in a compelling fashion. The main difference was this job paid better.

Even after Eli's accident, I'd continued to do freelance work for various papers and research projects for Carson to keep my sanity as well as provide a source of income. Sadly, that income over the years dropped to the point where I was barely making minimum wage for the time I put in. When papers and magazines were only paying forty dollars per article, when most of their stories were written by large overseas companies that threw together quick short articles and sold the rights to hundreds of news organizations across the globe, the local reporter found him or herself either without a job or writing for very little pay.

I wasn't going to get rich doing research for Pierson's, but the job was interesting, it paid the bills, and my boss was the stuff of sitcom reruns. J.T. Pierson had gotten his P.I. license as a young man fresh out of college with dreams of *Rockford Files* and *Magnum, P.I.* in his soul. His television role models had remained soundly in the seventies. He romanticized old-fashioned gumshoe detective work over modern CSI and internet research—which meant I had job security. J.T. went out to interview people, knock on doors, and liaison with the deputies serving warrants. I found people who didn't want to be found, building a paper trail that my boss would deposit on the DA's desk with a dramatic flourish.

"Did you see Snake last night? That guy has completely gone off the rails. He's gonna get shot one of these days."

No, I hadn't watched the latest episode of *Snake—Bounty Hunter*, J.T.'s newest reality show obsession. "What did he do this time? Stake out the wrong house? Fall asleep and let the perp slip away?"

"He tried to repo some guy's car out of his driveway, and the man showed up and blocked him in. Idiot."

Snake *was* an idiot, but idiots made for good reality television. Ever since the show had aired, J.T. was convinced that his future was with A&E, TLC, or some other channel. On Friday, he'd paid me overtime to stay late and research who he should submit his pitch to. It was his lifetime dream to see his investigative exploits on the small screen beside Jim Rockford and Thomas Magnum, and America's fixation with reality TV seemed like the perfect venue to launch a show of his own.

In preparation, he'd been experimenting with his "look." Last week's slovenly detective persona had been replaced over the weekend. Today J.T. was sporting jeans and a white t-shirt, along with cowboy boots that looked like he'd snipped the tags off them this morning. It wasn't just the clothing that was a total about-face from the week before either. J.T. had shaved his head.

For a man in his late fifties, J.T. had a decent amount of hair. Silver had been liberally sprinkled among the brown, and along with the increasing prominence of his forehead, he'd begun to suffer from the backside bald spot. He'd kept it a reasonable length and avoided the comb-over, although I suspected he'd used some hair product last week to achieve the disheveled look.

But now it was gone. All of it. The vast white expanse of flesh screamed for sunscreen, or a hat. It seemed J.T.'s envy of Snake the Repo Man had crossed into imitation of the man's dress and appearance. All he needed now was an arm full of colorful tattoos.

"What's on my list today?" I asked, trying to ignore the glare of fluorescent light off my boss's shiny head.

"Creditcorp has one—a garnishment they're trying to get served, and Bob asked if we could help with two of his bail jumpers."

Bob was an old friend and sometimes competitor of J.T.'s. His was a one-man office that specialized in providing bail bond services to the high-risk dealers and multiple offenders. He kept me almost as busy as J.T. did.

"Oh, and can you do some digging on our newest client?"

"Caryn Swanson?" Our local scandal had been released on bail on Friday. It seemed a little late to be checking up on her. Kind of like closing the barn door after you'd given the horse ten grand and let her trot on down the street.

"I know what you're thinking. She seemed a good risk—local business owner, besides the alleged prostitution ring, that is, family in Milford put up her ten percent without batting an eye. But last night I ran into Craig Walsh's secretary at the steakhouse and I bought her a few drinks."

Craig Walsh was Caryn Swanson's defense attorney. His

paralegal that J.T. insisted on calling a secretary was eighty if she was a day, and liked her gin. She was also sharp as a tack. J.T. sometimes got information from her, but I got the impression that she wound up with far more information than my boss at the end of those "chance" encounters.

"Yeah? What did Bonita tell you after a couple gimlets?"

J.T.'s brow furrowed. It made a line of wrinkles clear up to the top of his head. "Walsh can't find his client."

That was far more than the little tidbits of information Bonita usually shared. "Maybe she's in Milford staying with family? I'm sure it's got to be awkward staying in Locust Point right now with her arrest all over the papers and rumors running wild."

The brow wrinkles deepened. "No. She was supposed to meet him Sunday morning. When she didn't show, he went over to her place and checked with her family. No one knows where she is."

I'd admit the idea that one of our clients had run off on her bail was exciting. J.T. was worried about the money, but I was already thinking of passports to Mexico or a new identity in Wyoming. These sorts of things didn't happen in Locust Point. But then again, we didn't have arrests for a madam of a prostitution ring every day either.

"Want me to try to track her down?"

J.T. nodded, the frown easing somewhat. "Maybe she headed to the beach or something, but missing a meeting with her lawyer worries me. I just want to make sure I'm not going to be left holding the bag for ten grand."

"It would make a great episode on your show," I teased. "Me on the cell phone feeding you information while you are on a high-speed car chase with a warrant for Caryn Swanson's arrest."

Now my boss looked positively gleeful. "The folder with

the information on her is in the file. I added some notes. And I managed to get this."

I took the outstretched paper that J.T. handed me and looked it over. It was a copy of a police report—one that neither of us was supposed to be in possession of. I wasn't even sure Caryn's defense attorney had all of this.

"You've been working your own magic, I see."

J.T. reddened. He was a notorious flirt, and the emergency service operators loved him, as did the clerks at the courthouse. That and he'd been promising them all parts in his new reality TV series—the one he didn't have.

Caryn Swanson. Blonde. Green eyes. Five feet six. One ten. The arrest record was odd, not what I expected from someone who'd been caught up in a random undercover prostitution sting.

"What do you think?" I asked J.T. "You've got your ear to the pavement of the courthouse. Is she guilty? How did they catch her? Pimps and madams usually don't get caught through these undercover things."

According to my knowledge gained from years of investigative television shows, johns and hookers got caught in the stings. Pimps and madams were usually brought in through a longer investigation, turned in by a prostitute looking to bargain her way to a slap on the wrist and probation.

"There's a background investigation I don't have the details to. It's got to be in another case file somewhere. I'm assuming a few of her girls got arrested and turned her in, because this was clearly a setup." He gestured to the file.

I glanced at it briefly. Undercover officer communicates with suspect after contacting her through an online ad. She insists on a preliminary interview—huh, a bit classier than I'd expect. He gets enough information at the interview to arrest her for pandering. Maybe it was really this cut and dry.

Maybe Caryn Swanson was holed up at the beach drinking away the horrors of the weekend and trying to forget that she might be facing jail time. Maybe she was meeting right now with her lawyer, offering up her list of clients for a lighter sentence. Either way, I was going to spend some time today digging up everything I could find on this woman.

I put the folder in my stack next to the Creditcorp file. "Are you in the office today or out?"

"Out. I'm meeting with Pete Briscane this morning."

Our illustrious mayor. "Is he still trying to get you to sponsor a boat in the regatta?"

The wrinkles returned. "His son was in town this past weekend."

"Oh." The younger Briscane was trouble with a capital T. A few brushes with the law in high school, a few stints in rehab, a college that finally kicked him out in spite of the substantial donations his parents had made. They'd bought him a barbeque place on the shore a few years back, hoping to keep him busy and out of trouble—and hopefully take some responsibility. His restaurant was far enough that he wasn't on their doorstep every month, but close enough that they could keep an eye on him. That he was in town and that the mayor wanted to talk to J.T. probably meant David was in trouble once more—in enough trouble to potentially require bail or investigative services.

I added a mental note to check into David Briscane's barbeque joint and finances. Yes, that made me just as much of a snoop as Daisy and J.T.... I'd blame it on my investigative journalist past, but honestly, I was curious. And a snoop.

I logged on and waved J.T. out the door, adding Briscane's name to my list. I had a lot to do today, but even if I had to skip lunch and make do with the scone in my purse, I was going to see what I could find on Caryn Swanson and do some digging on the mayor's notorious son.

CHAPTER 9

I never got to David Briscane. The Creditcorp subject had just started a job as a third-shift cashier at the Gas N Go. He wouldn't make enough there to allow much for the judgment, but there was evidence that a local construction company was paying him as a contractor —cash, judging from the regular Friday-night deposits into his bank account. I was willing to bet the man kept most of the payment under his mattress, depositing just enough to cover the automatic payments for his cable television and internet service.

That done, I wolfed down my scone and tried to see what I could find on Caryn Swanson. At twenty-three, the girl's credit history was a rollercoaster of on-time and late payments. There was nothing on the state case search beyond a speeding ticket she'd received last year. The employment history on her Social Security number showed the party-planner job. She made good money there, but when I put everything together, a pattern revealed itself.

Two years ago, her credit stabilized and small steady cash deposits began. At the end of last year, she paid for a car in cash—as in cash-cash, not a check. Admittedly, it wasn't a luxury car, but most people didn't carry around thousands for a used sedan.

But plenty of people did under-the-table work, including the Gas N Go guy I'd just finished tracing. I wasn't accusing him of running a prostitution ring. And honestly, Caryn Swanson's guilt or innocence wasn't my job. Finding out where she'd run off to was.

Which meant I needed to go outside her credit reports and bank records. I turned to the research avenues that yielded my biggest results—social media. Nothing was private anymore, regardless of how people managed their security settings. I'd long since stopped being shocked at the detail of information humans put out for public consumption. It wasn't unusual to see illegal activity splashed across Facebook or documented in Instagram photos.

And unlike us old folk, people today seemed to be unbothered by the need to keep *anything* private. Sure enough, Caryn Swanson's life was laid out for all the world to see—beach pictures, holiday shots, guzzling a beer by a pool, flashing cleavage, and making duck-lips for the camera. She also had a business page with tons of photos from her various weddings, graduation parties, and anniversary celebrations. Nothing had been posted on either since her arrest. I downloaded all sorts of pictures from her personal account, complete with who was tagged, and the location of where each was taken as well as the time and date of post. I'd check these out later for a list of Caryn's buddies who might have given her a safe harbor away from the publicity.

Snapchat was loaded with messages asking what was going on and less-than-subtle digs for details behind obvious curiosity. I copied down contacts and messages to cross reference with the Facebook posts.

In a way, all this online activity made my job harder. It

took me hours to wade through the metric ton of selfies and party posts to get any kind of grasp on who Caryn Swanson's friends were and who were just casual acquaintances.

There was one other thing missing from her online persona. I would have overlooked it if I hadn't waded back through two years of mind-numbing posts and pictures. Caryn Swanson, as beautiful and sexy as she seemed to be, didn't have a boyfriend. There were all sorts of less-than-subtle snide remarks about who I assumed was an ex from when she would have been eighteen, then there was nothing —nothing except party pics and business photos.

It seemed odd, but it had been a long time since I'd been a young woman and I honestly didn't know how the dating world worked nowadays. Paging forward, I returned to the posts right before her arrest that might shed light on where Caryn had been over the weekend, and where she was now. Twitter and Snapchat held the most recent pictures, so I downloaded them and opened them up on my gigantic monitor, enlarging and photo enhancing what I could.

Nothing indicated she had been planning a trip to Ocean City, New York, or any road trips. There were some party pictures from the weekend before, posted right around sundown, but nothing afterward. It was better than nothing. I zoomed in on the party pictures, determined to find out where it had been held and who else was in attendance. Someone had to have known where Caryn had run off to.

That's when I saw a familiar face. I don't know a lot of teenagers, but this one had been in my house as of yesterday, and I would have recognized her anywhere. It was Madison Beck, the judge's fifteen-year-old daughter. She was wearing a pair of toddler-sized booty shorts, what looked like a bandana across her chest, and she was holding a signature red Solo cup. There was the shiny silver of a keg off to the side. She wasn't the focus of the picture, of course. But Madison was clearly visible off to the back.

She'd been busted by a photo bomb. While drinking beer at a party. I would have to tell her father. I really didn't want to. Yes, I'd done similar stuff, although I didn't remember drinking beer at fifteen, but that wasn't why I was squirming in my ergonomic office chair at the thought of the conversation I was going to have later—it was the drama that conversation would cause. There would be crying and yelling, and a teenage girl grounded in a bedroom of my home. Plus, the judge would blame his wife who'd been responsible for the kids that Saturday night. It was going to be so ugly, and I hated ugly, but he had to know—and I had to talk to Madison. She'd been at this party with Caryn. I'd still give J.T. a list of contacts who had been tagged in other photos, but if Caryn was still missing, Madison might know where she was, or at least who she was with.

CHAPTER 10

I left J.T. a message with the typed summaries of both the Creditcorp job and what I'd dug up so far on Caryn. What I hadn't done was let my boss know about Madison Beck's presence at the party. The picture was in the file, although I didn't think J.T. had ever met the girl or would be able to identify her from the picture. My loyalty to J.T. didn't extend far enough to let him turn Madison Beck into the latest town gossip, especially not before either of her parents knew and had a chance to confront her themselves.

Plus, I wanted to talk with her first. I got the impression that the girl might be more open to telling me about the party rather than J.T.—or probably even her own Dad—although I had no illusions that she'd be warm and friendly, given that I was about to rat her out.

The judge, true to his word, had picked both kids up from school. By the time I got home, the two teens were at the dining room table, books and notepads spread all over the surface as they did their homework. I heard the bang of pots in the kitchen and smelled the heavenly aroma of bacon and beef. Whatever my new roomie was cooking up, I was willing to bet it was a whole lot tastier than the salad I had in the fridge.

"Can I speak to you for a quick second?" I asked Madison. She looked up from her homework with surprise.

"Sure."

I led her off to the side room that had once housed Eli's bed and pulled the photo from my briefcase, laying it on the back of the sofa for her to see.

She sucked in a breath. "Where...when...? Someone photoshopped that because it's not me."

"It's not photoshopped. I had to enlarge it for this close up." I pulled the print of the original out and sat it beside the other. This one had Caryn Swanson front and center, Madison just a figure in the back near the keg.

"Are you spying on me?" Her voice rose, then lowered with a quick look back at the dining room. "Why do you have these pictures?"

"I do research for a bail-bond firm, and we're just making sure Caryn Swanson doesn't skip out on her bail." I let that sink in for a moment. "We think she might have gone away with a friend this past weekend. We need to reach her, so I'm trying to find out who her friends are, who she might have gone out of town with. And I'm hoping since you were at this party you might know."

Madison rubbed her hands over her face. "Are you going to tell Dad? I was supposed to be at Chelsea's. We were the only two there who weren't in our twenties. I couldn't even believe I was invited. Please don't tell Dad."

She was more concerned about getting grounded than me finding out where Caryn was. Teens. Although honestly, being caught at a party with a woman who'd been arrested for running a prostitution ring was probably a far more serious offense than just a run-of-the-mill teenage party.

"I have to tell your father. These pictures are on Caryn

Swanson's social media. They'll most likely be introduced as part of her court case. Can you imagine what's going to happen if your dad is serving on this trial and sees a party picture with his daughter in the background next to a keg?"

She crumpled and I held back the urge to wrap my arms around her. "He's going to kill me. He'll kill me. Then he'll kill Mom. He'll blame her for this whole thing."

Probably. Well, the blaming Heather, not the killing.

"I won't lie, you're going to be in some serious trouble, but he won't kill you and you'll be better off letting him know now than if he were blindsided in the middle of a trial."

She nodded, then took a breath to compose herself. "I didn't know about the prostitution stuff. I swear I didn't know, and I'm not sure I believe it. Chelsea's sister knows her. Caryn did her graduation party a few years back. They're not big friends or anything, but they kind of run in the same social circles. Locust Point is small. They hang out at the same places.

"Anyway, Leah knew about the party and asked if Chelsea wanted to come. Chelsea felt weird about being at a party with people that much older than us, so she asked me to come along. It was fun. I didn't get drunk or anything. There weren't any drugs, and the guys there were nice. Cute. But they didn't try to hit on us or anything. It was like we were their little sisters or something."

"Little sisters who drink beer from kegs and are practically naked."

"My bathing suit covers less than that," Madison shot back.

"It's March. And you're not at a pool."

She glared silently at me after that. I needed to back off. She wasn't my kid, and I needed her to give me information. She'd hate me enough once I showed her father this picture.

"So Chelsea's sister, Leah, is Caryn's friend?"

"No, not really. They just run into each other at parties and stuff. Leah probably knows her friends, though."

And Leah might know who would have the inside information on where Caryn had gone. If she was still missing, that is. I was going to wring J.T.'s neck if I'd gone to all this trouble only to find that she'd missed the meeting with her lawyer because she was hungover.

"And what are Leah and Chelsea's names?"

"Novak."

"Thanks." I nodded. "I'm going to talk to your father."

She nodded, her eyes huge. "I'm so dead. Dead. Dad is gonna kill me. He's gonna kill me, then Mom is gonna kill me."

I patted her on the shoulder. "I'll see if I can't get him to kill you a little less than he normally would."

I left her at the dining room table, hands shaking as she worked on her homework. Then I went into the kitchen. Judge Beck still had on his work pants, his shirt partially unbuttoned and sleeves rolled up. His jacket and tie were draped over the back of a chair. Grease was splattered all over my cooktop from the bacon cheeseburgers in a frying pan.

I didn't know how to ease into this, so I just jumped right in. "Pierson did the bail for Caryn Swanson and I did some research on her today. There are worries that she may have run off, that she might be a flight risk."

The judge looked up in surprise, spatula in hand. "For those charges? Why? She'd probably wind up with a slap on the wrist if she turns over the client list."

"I don't know. It's a small town. Even if it's knocked down to a lesser charge, her party planning business is over. Maybe she's looking into starting over somewhere else."

He looked over at me, spatula dripping grease on the floor. "Has she left town? I know Pierson wouldn't have you digging into this if she was home safe. If he was worried about her leaving, he would have checked this out before posting her bail, so she must be missing?"

I sighed. Might as well gossip like the rest of the town. "Yeah. She probably ran off to the beach with a friend to get away from all of this, but J.T. is worried she might have bolted."

"She empty her bank account?" The judge flipped a burger.

"No." Where was he going with this?

"She's not going to run off on what will probably end up being a minor charge with her car and the clothes on her back. That's why the bail is so low. If she was up for murder, if she was connected to organized crime or a drug cartel, *that's* when I expect her to bolt. Not over this."

My blood suddenly ran cold. I blame it on too many thrillers and those late-night television mysteries. What if there was something—someone—in that little black book who really didn't want to be exposed?

"Does Walsh know where she is? I'm assuming that gin-swilling paralegal of his tipped off Pierson."

Hey. That was uncalled for. True, but uncalled for.

"Don't underestimate Bonita. She might like her gin, but I wouldn't call her a lush."

I suddenly remembered the judge seeing Daisy and I drinking enormous glasses of wine on the porch. Did he think *I* was a lush? Was I going to need to sneak around my own house, just so my roommate didn't condemn me for what his puritanical self might consider over-indulgence?

"I'll take that as a yes. So if Walsh thinks she's missing, why hasn't he filed a police report?"

"I don't know. Maybe he doesn't want even more of a dust-up over the woman if she just went off the grid for the weekend."

He shrugged. "I think you're wasting your time. She'll turn up. And once this all blows over, she'll eventually be able to rebuild her business—the legal one, that is. Unless your research revealed a secret bank account in the Cayman Islands, I think J.T.'s investment is safe."

He slid the burgers on the plate and put the pan in the sink. I wasn't sure how to bridge between the conversation about Caryn Swanson and Madison, but I needed to tell him. Now. Not after dinner.

"Actually, I need to speak to you about something else. Something related, but not really. It might come up in the trial, so I thought you should know." I was rambling incoherently, dreading the blowup that would follow.

"Yeah?" He hesitated, plate of burgers in one hand.

I pulled the pictures out of the folder and sat them on the island counter—one showing Caryn Swanson at a party, the other the enlargement showing Madison by the keg.

"If there were clients at this party, or some of the prostitutes, then these pictures are going to be part of the trial. I wanted to make sure you saw this first. Before the trial."

He sat the plate of burgers down and stared at the photos, a muscle in his jaw twitching. "When was this taken?"

"A week ago Saturday. I spoke to Madison about it just now because I'm trying to track down Caryn's friends. She knows I'm telling you about it."

Judge Beck inhaled. It was a ragged breath, as if his throat were closing up. "My daughter was at a party last Saturday night. She was at a party with these much older kids, one of them arrested for running a prostitution ring, a party where there might have been johns and prostitutes. She was at this party holding a cup of what I suspect is beer."

His voice was numb, wooden. Then he looked up at me and his eyes blazed. "I'm going to kill Heather for this. How could she let this happen? She wants to deny me half custody, and our daughter is out drinking and partying with people in their mid-twenties, with prostitutes, on *her* watch?"

"Well, we don't know for sure that there were prostitutes or johns at the party," I hastily interjected. This was not going well. I hadn't expected it to go well, but the reality of his anger was so upsetting. "We don't even know if Caryn Swanson is guilty."

"It's *my* daughter," he snarled. "My fifteen-year-old daughter partying and drinking beer with people ten years older than her. I don't care whether Caryn Swanson is guilty or not, my daughter is too young to be at this sort of thing."

I took a step back, worried that he was going to do something violent with that spatula. It probably wasn't the right time to remind him that we'd all snuck out at that age. Well, I assumed he had, too. He might be a judge now, but I didn't get the impression that he'd obeyed every rule when young. Honestly, he probably didn't even obey every rule now.

He threw the spatula across the room, where it clattered off the end of the counter and across the floor. "What was Heather doing while my daughter was getting drunk and who knows what else at a party? Out with Tyler? Did she ditch Henry with a sitter, or send him off to a friend so she could run around like an irresponsible tramp? She's probably clueless about what the kids do in the evenings. She's completely unfit to have any custody at all."

This was bad. So bad. I wanted to hide under the table or grab Taco and lock myself in my room. It was as if I were Madison, if I were Heather and guilty in all this instead of just the messenger.

I couldn't hide, though. I needed to live with this guy, live most of the time with his kids, and see his soon-to-be-ex-wife several times a week. I had to ride this very unpleasant emotional moment out. Then I'd get Taco and hide in my room. Maybe with a bottle of wine.

"Stop it. Stop it now. Kids are sneaky, and as much as you want to blame Heather, don't blow this out of proportion. Madison said she was supposed to be spending the night at Chelsea's. Would you have followed up? Would you have doubted her?"

The judge hesitated. "Chelsea is one of Madison's friends. She's a good girl, gets good grades. We played golf with her parents. No, I probably wouldn't have doubted her, but I will now."

"Then have an adult parenting discussion with Heather. Tell her what happened, and between the two of you come up with a way to ensure this doesn't happen again. Madison knows she's lost your trust. She won't be surprised if you doubt her, if you follow up on her overnights or after-school activities, going forward."

He glanced over at the spatula on the floor and suddenly looked embarrassed. "I'm so angry at Madison for this. She's too smart to make these kind of dumb decisions. Maybe if she was seventeen or eighteen, I would have expected this sort of thing, but *fifteen?*"

He was right. She was young, but kids seemed to do things at such a younger age than we did. Well, then *I* did. "She didn't know that Caryn was about to be arrested for being a madam, she didn't even know Caryn at all. Chelsea's older sister invited her to the party, and she didn't want to go without someone else her age, so she asked Madison to go along. There was alcohol, but she swears there were no drugs and the guys were respectful, they treated them like kid sisters."

The judge caught his breath. "Oh, God. What if there *had* been drugs? What if one of those guys had slipped her something, then raped her?"

"That didn't happen. She lied and went to a party. She drank beer. Teens do this sort of thing. You're going to make sure it doesn't happen again, at least until she goes off to college."

I probably shouldn't have said that last part, even though it was true.

"I might not be able to control what she does in college, but I'm going to make sure she's not sneaking out to parties and drinking alcohol while she's a minor under my roof. I'm not going to sweep this under the rug." He scowled.

"I don't expect you to," I hastily replied. It wasn't my business. I'd told him, now it was up to him to deal with his daughter and his ex-wife. He didn't need, or probably want, further comments from me.

He sighed, running a hand over top of his dark hair. "Lots of teens make this mistake and lots of teens end up dead in car accidents, in the hospital for a drug or alcohol overdose, or raped. I don't want to get that phone call. She's... she's my baby girl."

His voice choked and I felt tears sting my eyes at the emotion in his words. It was every parent's worst fear. I could only envision how hard it was to watch your little ones grow up and hope every time they left your arms that they returned safely again.

"I know, and I can't begin to imagine how that feels."

He nodded and turned back to pick up the plate of burgers. "I'll talk to her after dinner."

There was no offer of a burger for me, and given how tense their dinner would most likely be, I was actually glad to pull my salad out of the fridge and eat elsewhere. I figured it was a good time to take my food outside and enjoy the spring evening, away from the storm brewing in my house.

CHAPTER 11

J.T. went through my notes a second time. "She's definitely gone. Out of all the bonds I've posted, I never would have guessed this would be the one I would have to track down."

"What do you need me to do?" J.T. would most likely handle questioning the Facebook and Snapchat friends. I was a bit reluctant to give up Madison's friend and her sister, especially given that the girl had said they barely knew Caryn. Maybe if these other leads didn't turn up anything, I'd check with them. I hated to whack that bee's nest again.

"See what else you can find. Any kind of credit card trail, anything. Being accused of running a prostitution ring isn't enough to get her more than the most basic police interest, so finding her is going to be up to us."

"I'm on it," I announced, sitting down at my computer. An hour later, and I'd discovered scant else about Caryn Swanson. She had graduated from Locust Point High School. She had gone to Milford County Community College, then on to the state college, graduating two years ago with a business degree. Her parents had loaned her the money to start her party planner business, and it had been enough of a success that she'd paid them back within six months.

From all the pictures, the website, and the recommendations, she seemed to be a good business woman. She'd had quite a lot of success for someone her age. Was she truly innocent? Some kinky girl who had mistakenly gotten caught in a sting? No, there had to be something behind the charges, or she would have just been up for prostitution. There had to be a reason the police were so eager to get their hands on that black book.

It was one o'clock before I realized that I hadn't brought anything for lunch. If I was going to run out, I might as well swing by the grocery store and grab something to cook for dinner. And some baking supplies. It would be nice if the breakfast pastries that I shared with Daisy each morning weren't store bought. I used to love to bake. It was something I wanted to pick up again. And if I made two coffee cakes instead of one, then perhaps those two kids wouldn't have to eat frosted donuts and frozen waffles for breakfast.

MegaMart was fairly empty but I still parked in the back as far from the doors as I could, determined to get a little exercise in as I always did. As soon as I hopped out of my car, I felt an icy chill and saw a shadow out of the corner of my eye.

I'd forgotten about the shadow, or floater, or whatever the ophthalmologist had called it. The visions hadn't reoccurred since Sunday night, when I'd been downstairs watching movies.

I turned, expecting the dark shadow to vanish as always. This time it stayed, an indistinct, gray figure in the center of my vision. It was like seeing a ghost. Well, it was like what I imagined seeing a ghost would be like, except not in broad daylight at the edge of a MegaMart parking lot. Was there something seriously wrong with my eyesight? Did I need to see the ophthalmologist again?

The shadow paced, then headed over to the grassy section between the parking lot and the highway, the huge patch of briars and weeds that down a ten-foot embankment hid a drainage ditch. There it hovered, floating and twisting in the air, one long appendage stretched outward, as if beseeching me to do something.

Do what? Get sunglasses? See an eye doctor? I blinked hard a few times and rubbed my eyes, but the shadow was still there. Pointing. Reaching toward me.

And then it was gone. The air turned warm and I heard birdsong that had been unusually silent just a moment before.

What was that? A trick of the light? My cataract surgery gone horribly wrong? Feeling like a total fool, I walked carefully across the broken edge of asphalt toward the area where I'd seen the shadow. The briars and grasses near the edge of the parking lot looked crushed. Had someone been here? Homeless people used to have some tents in this spot when it had been more wooded and before the MegaMart had come. Now it was just a bunch of weeds and a steep hill down to the drainage pond. I couldn't even imagine using it as a cut-through to the truck stop since any pedestrian would need to navigate this bramble-filled slope, skirt the wet pond area, then cross six lanes of interstate. I was just about to turn around and leave when I saw something in the weeds—something blue and shiny. Reaching down, I pulled it free.

A shoe. A woman's blue pump. It hadn't been here long from the look of it. What woman loses a perfectly good shoe? A rather attractive shoe? And just one of them? My imagination went into overdrive and I peered down the slope to the drainage pond, trying to see if there was anything down there.

A body? It would be the perfect place to dump a body. Or it would be the perfect place for some drunk woman to fall and lose her shoe in the middle of the night. I was such an idiot. It was a shoe. And I was seeing floaters from my cataract surgery.

Yes, I was an idiot because I was going to risk breaking my neck to check this out. Maybe I'd luck out and find the mate to this shoe. Maybe I'd luck out and they'd be my size.

It was April. The pond would have a good bit of water in it. And judging from the two-foot grass that grew up around it, the area was never mowed. I was willing to believe it was never bothered with at all. I walked around the edge where asphalt met grass, trying to find the best spot to descend. I saw a few bags of trash and an old window air-conditioning unit—left by someone who didn't want to pay the landfill fees at the dump, no doubt. I also saw a trail of smashed grass that looked a bit more level than the other spots.

I mulled through the scenarios as I carefully climbed down the pathway. I was certain a woman in high heels couldn't navigate this path. If the owner of this shoe had been drunk and fallen, how far would she have rolled? I envisioned the girl falling with the first step of her high heels in the soft ground, tumbling down to the bottom of the steep hill, and possibly plunging into the edge of the pond. It wasn't terribly deep, but the grasses grew thick and tall right up to the edge. If she'd hit her head on a rock...

I hesitated, my own shoes soggy in the mud. This was ridiculous. I'd seen a shadow. I'd found a shoe. And here I was climbing down a muddy, weed-infested hill with that shoe in hand. *My* shoes might be forever ruined, and I'd need a whole lot of pre-soak to get the mud out of the hem of my pants, but I had to know. Taking a deep breath, I kept going, hearing the mud suck up around my feet with each step. After about five yards I saw it—another shoe. It was a blue patent shoe, a match to the one I held. I stooped down to look at it, afraid to pick it up. Would I fall on my face down into the pond? Would quicksand pull me into the ground? And there was another reason I was afraid to pick it up.

It wasn't just a shoe. I knew in my heart there was more, and I really didn't want to keep going. But I couldn't call the police and tell them that I'd seen a shadow in a parking lot, and I couldn't tell them that I'd found a shoe at the bottom of a grassy median between said parking lot and the highway. They'd assume it had been tossed here as a prank. I needed more than a shoe, so I went on.

I found more. Just a few steps away, facedown in the pond and surrounded by weeds, I found what I'd feared to find.

CHAPTER 12

The police had cordoned off the pond and the parking lot, roping my car in along with the rest of the evidence. There were three squad cars, the M.E., an ambulance, and J.T. My boss paced back and forth, stopping occasionally to look down the hill at the little numbered markers and the body covered in plastic. As for me, I couldn't tear my eyes away.

In all my years as a reporter, I'd never seen a dead person. Yes, I'd been there when Eli passed away, but I hadn't seen him days later after his body had been half-submerged in water. This was horrific. Eli's death had been peaceful, serene. This woman's was anything but that.

"Do you think it's her?" I asked J.T.

He glanced down at the tarp. "I'm assuming so. Blonde. She's the right age. It's not like there are any other missing persons in Locust Point."

"Maybe it's someone from out of town," I said. "Maybe she was traveling on the interstate, pulled into the truck stop, got drunk, fell down the hill, and drowned."

J.T. shot me a look that clearly said I was crazy. "She got

drunk at the truck stop, crossed six lanes of traffic and climbed through the ditch to the parking lot, lost her shoe, then fell trying to get back down?"

Okay, he was right. That didn't make sense at all. "She's drunk at the truck stop. She hooks up with some guy who drives her over here for car sex in a parking lot after hours. Afterward, she falls down the ditch and drowns trying to get back to the truck stop."

J.T. considered my theory. "Well, if that's true, then some jerk drove her here to have sex with her, then left her, drunk and alone, in a dark parking lot."

About that time, one of the deputies climbed up the hill to us. "Looks like that Swanson woman to me. It hasn't been that warm the last few days, but she was facedown in the water, so we'll want to wait for the M.E. report before we announce the victim's ID."

Which was code for keep your mouths shut.

J.T. shook his head. "I want to give Craig Walsh the heads-up, just in case. She got out on bail Friday morning and didn't show up for a meeting with him Saturday afternoon, so if it's Caryn Swanson in that bag, that should narrow down the time of death."

The deputy shrugged. "I guess that won't hurt. I'm going to rush an identification, just so we can let everyone know. I'm sure it's all over town that we found a body."

We all looked up at the overpass above the interstate where cars were parked and people were lined up, gawking and taking cell phone pictures. Yeah. Small town excitement. First a prostitution arrest, and now a body behind the MegaMart.

"Do you think..." I wasn't sure I wanted to know, but part of me did. "Do you think it was an accident, or that she was murdered?"

The deputy's expression suddenly became completely

blank. It was the best poker face I'd ever seen. "No idea. We'll need to wait for the M.E.'s report."

Which meant he assumed murder. I assumed murder; although, to be fair, she could have stumbled down the hill drunk and drowned. But if that was the case, where was her car? Did she walk here? There was nowhere nearby that she could walk from. As J.T. had said, the truck stop was either a mile up and over the interstate bridge in those pretty blue patent shoes, or she'd parked somewhere in the MegaMart parking lot. But if she'd parked up near the front of the store, why in the world would she have come back here?

I hated to even think it, but murder was the only thing that made sense. And there was only one reason I could think of for someone to murder Caryn Swanson.

What *was* in that black book?

CHAPTER 13

$\mathcal{I}$ headed straight home, figuring I could finish my work from there. I'd forgotten all about the baking supplies and the pork loin, but wasn't feeling particularly hungry anyway. Once home, I pulled the files out of my briefcase and stared at them. Murder. It had to have been murder.

If the black book was the key to this, the tell-all list of clients, we might never find it now. The best suspect for murdering Caryn Swanson would be someone on that list that didn't want to be exposed. He probably either had the book, or Caryn had hidden it somewhere we'd never find.

But just because the book might be gone, it didn't mean I couldn't trace her clients from the other direction.

I pulled up several internet sites that had dating sections. I knew full well that no amount of regulation would keep interested parties from listing and looking for prostitutes of either sex on these sites. I narrowed down the zip code search a bit, then started looking through the listings. What I saw made me want to wash my eyes out with Clorox. It was very clear that just about anything could be had for a certain, unnamed and vaguely alluded to, price. I wrote down the ones that looked promising along with their messaging ID. I wasn't a hacker, so there was no way I could find out who owned those IDs without a warrant, but I could check one more thing. Four of the ten had websites. They weren't anything special, but they'd do. I pinged the URL, then used a lookup on the IP address. None of the four were anywhere near Locust Point. I doubted that Caryn Swanson would have driven two hours out of town to run her website, so I went on to the other six.

"There's more than one way to skin a cat," I muttered, sending a silent apology to Taco. Composing what I hoped were messages a prospective client might send a service, I e-mailed all six. Two sent back an auto-respond so I pulled up the IP address from the header and ran a WHOIS check and a geolocation.

And there it was, Locust Point. I wrote down the information and did a screenshot of the dating-site ad, then sat back in my chair. Next, I'd use search engine analytics to find out where this IP had been visiting online. It might yield something, it might not. I might wind up finding out that Caryn Swanson bought shoes online and searched websites for how to remove warts or something. It would need to wait, though. I was tired. Finding a dead body took a lot out of a person.

I went to pack the folder away and a slip of paper fell onto my lap. *David Briscane*. The mayor's son. I was beat, and snooping around for this guy's misdeeds wasn't really a priority, but I couldn't help at least running a state case search.

Oh my. Poor Mayor Briscane. It seems his son was in quite a bit of debt by the pending civil suits and judgments. A drunk driving charge, too. I closed my browser and turned off the computer, feeling a bit sorry for our mayor. No doubt his son was in town asking for money. Sad, but Locust Point had bigger problems right now than the mayor's reprobate child.

I organized my notes on Caryn Swanson and by the time I'd stuffed the folder back into my briefcase, Judge Beck was walking through the door with his two kids in tow. Three, as the group included a girl I hadn't seen before. Madison, head down, walked straight up the stairs, heading I'm sure toward her bedroom. The girl followed. Henry hesitated, looking at the dining room table then after his sister, choosing the latter and also heading up the stairs.

I watched them go, chewing my bottom lip and wondering if Madison Beck would ever speak to me again. It wasn't my fault she was in trouble, but I was the one who discovered the photo and told her father. I'm sure she blamed me for the whole thing. Hopefully in time she'd come around; otherwise, we'd both be in for an awkward two years.

CHAPTER 14

*J*udge Beck stood in the hallway for a few minutes watching his kids go upstairs, then he wandered into my study and stopped in the doorway. His eyes met mine and I knew he wanted to talk. So did I. I stood and walked to the kitchen. He followed. Without asking, I pulled two wine glasses from the cabinet and yanked the cork from a bottle of Pinot Grigio that had been in the fridge from Daisy's and my indulgence over the weekend.

"She's grounded for the week. If you have any chores you'd like her to do around the house, I can add them to the punishment. I'm afraid things might be a bit frosty around here for a while, but she'll get over it."

I handed him a glass of wine. "I found a body today."

His mouth dropped open. "What? You what? I don't think I heard that right because it sounded like you said you found a body."

I nodded. "A dead body. In that drainage ditch that separates the MegaMart parking lot from the interstate. She'd been there a few days. No ID yet, but we're thinking it may be Caryn Swanson."

Judge Beck stared at me a moment, downed the wine, then handed the glass back to me. I gave him a refill. "I'm not supposed to tell anyone, but you're a judge. I know you'll keep your mouth shut on it. I *had* to tell someone. I love Daisy to pieces, but she'd have this all over town in five minutes."

He sat the wine down and rubbed his face. "How did you find her?"

How to explain this without getting into the fact that I was either going crazy, or my eyesight had some serious problems? "I always park back there to get some exercise. I saw a shoe in the brush at the edge of the parking lot—a nice shoe that looked like it had been left there recently. I went down the hill to the drainage pond to see..." Drat, how do I make this sound like something a reasonable woman would do? "If I could find the other shoe."

He stared at me. "You hiked down a rocky, briar-choked hill into the mud and a water-filled drainage ditch to see if you could find the other shoe? How nice was that shoe? I mean, are we talking six hundred dollar shoes here, or something?"

I sounded like a complete idiot. "No, it was just a nice shoe, not the sort of thing someone would just throw away at the end of a parking lot. The grass was trampled, like there was a path, so I thought maybe someone had fallen down the hill and needed help." There. That was a better reason than me scavenging for shoes.

"Kay, what were you thinking? Homeless people used to live there. What if someone jumped you and robbed you? What if you were the one that fell and twisted your ankle, or knocked yourself out on a rock?"

"I was in clear view of the interstate in broad daylight. The homeless people moved out when the MegaMart went in and they tore down the trees, and they were just homeless people, not thugs. If I fell, I had my cell phone. It's not like I'm some old lady hobbling around. I take walks. I do yoga." I get that he was probably still dwelling on Madison sneaking out to a party, but I was *not* his underage daughter for him to fuss over like this. Had he treated Heather this way? If so, then my sympathies in this divorce were leaning in her direction.

"Sorry. I had a domestic violence case today. Between that and Madison, I'm overestimating the danger of pretty much everything right now." He looked down at the wine, as if he were weighing whether to drink it or stop at the one glass he'd treated like a shot of tequila. "Was her car back there? Was it an overdose? Suicide? A drunken accident?"

"Her car wasn't back there and I'm assuming she didn't have any ID on her if the police are waiting to announce it. They didn't tell us what they were thinking in terms of cause of death, but I'm leaning toward murder."

That got him drinking the second glass of wine. Thankfully, he wasn't throwing this one down his throat. "Murder? How do you get murder? She was accused of running a minor prostitution ring and out on bail. There was nothing in that case that would have caused her to be killed. Otherwise Walsh would have brought it up at the bail hearing."

"She was reluctant to release her list of contacts, even though she would most likely have gotten a reduced sentence or even probation."

He shrugged. "She was holding out for a better deal. Walsh was still negotiating with the prosecution."

I shook my head. "Walsh didn't have a counter offer. He was sticking fast with the innocent plea."

"Drugs, then. She was shooting up back there, passed out,

lost one of her shoes and rolled down the hill and died either of an overdose or by drowning while passed out."

"There was no history of drugs. There wasn't even a rumor of drugs, and you know what this town is like. She was clean when she was arrested. You can't tell me she got out on bail and suddenly decided to go shoot up with heroin completely alone in the back of a parking lot?"

"Not alone. That's why her car wasn't there. The junkie with her saw her fall and took off."

Oh, for Pete's sake. "A junkie would most likely have laughed at her falling down the hill, then passed out in her car. She was supposed to meet with her attorney on Saturday afternoon, but didn't show. She gets out of jail on Friday and most likely winds up dead that night. Bit of a stretch to call that a coincidence."

He took another drink of wine. "Coincidences happen. She celebrates her release from jail. Drinks too much. Falls down the ditch and drowns."

I was going to shake this man. Shake him. "So instead of drinking with friends or in a bar, a successful party planner goes to the back of a parking lot in a remote area, imbibes a bottle of something, then falls and dies. And somehow the empty bottle and her car mysteriously drive off on their own?"

"She wasn't murdered. That's an insane theory, Kay. And we don't even know for sure it was Caryn Swanson. For all we know that poor dead woman is a truck stop pickup that got ditched by her one-night stand and died trying to take a short cut back across the interstate."

That was J.T.'s idea, but I knew better. "Murder. Caryn Swanson. I'll bet you I'm right."

I winced as soon as it came out of my mouth. Betting on the identity and cause of death of a woman who'd lost her life was so callous. Evidently a career of seeing criminals every day had jaded Judge Beck, because he didn't appear shocked at my terribly inappropriate suggestion of a wager.

"You're on. If you're right, I'll cook dinner. If I'm right, then you have to take Madison clothes shopping this weekend in my stead."

I remembered the hamburgers from last night and didn't think that was an equitable reward, but I'd take it. And losing the bet wouldn't really be a loss since I hated the idea of Caryn Swanson being murdered, and clothes shopping with Madison sounded fun. Well, if she was speaking to me by then, that is.

"Deal."

No sooner had we clinked our wine glasses to seal the deal than my phone buzzed. I looked down at it, then turned to show Judge Beck the text message.

It was Caryn Swanson. She was strangled.

I'd just won a bet. And winning that particular bet made me feel sick. There was more than a prostitution ring in our sleepy little town.

There was a murderer.

CHAPTER 15

*D*aisy and I had coffee and the last of the scones the next morning after our sunrise yoga. I hadn't gotten my baking supplies as planned, nor my pork roast. I'd need to go to the grocery store today, but I was thinking of driving to another one on the other side of town to avoid memories of yesterday. Although it wasn't like I was thinking of much else. Perhaps if I went there and just parked elsewhere, I wouldn't find myself thinking of a woman's body facedown in a ditch, her long blonde hair muddy and tangled in the weeds.

I'd declined Judge Beck's offer to share in their pizza last night and taken a rain check instead. I'd just needed the night to myself, so I'd slipped out for barbeque with a novel stuffed in my purse, coming home after everyone was upstairs for the night. My floater was back. I could see him out of the corner of my eye, as if he were sitting next to me in the booth at dinner, and across the room as I got ready for bed. Instead of the usual annoyance, I felt somewhat comforted by the shadowy presence. I honestly felt it helped me sleep soundly, even after the day's upsetting events.

This morning, there were signs that Judge Beck had been down for a cup of coffee before I'd awakened, but no sign of the man himself, or his two kids yet.

That poor woman dead. So young. She'd had her whole life ahead of her. Even if she'd been found guilty, she would have recovered. The whole thing would have faded away in a few years, of no more importance than Jess Bart's three DWI's and Billy Cowden's indecent exposure arrest that time he'd peed in the City Hall fountain five years ago. Instead of a temporary disgrace, she was dead. And I couldn't stop seeing her corpse in my mind.

After our relaxing yoga, Daisy didn't hesitate to bring the whole thing back to the forefront of my mind.

"Did you read the paper this morning? Can you believe it? Who do you think did it?" Daisy always read the news online before coming over. Since I waited for my actual paper to be delivered, I hadn't read the news, but I still knew exactly what she was talking about.

"Yes. I'm assuming one of her clients doesn't want to be exposed."

"She wasn't going to turn over her black book, from what I heard. Do you think she was blackmailing him? That would be a good reason to kill her. And she'd hardly want to turn over her client list and cut off a source of blackmail income."

Wow. Daisy's mind was just as twisted as mine. "Maybe she was blackmailing him, but met with him Friday night to tell him she had to go public with the list. Blackmail money doesn't do a lot of good in jail, and I heard they were offering her a really good plea bargain."

"Makes you think," Daisy mused, taking a sip of her coffee. "Why would the police care that much about the client list? I could see reduced jail time, but it would have to be something that pretty much got her off completely for her to expose someone she'd been blackmailing. And somebody the police really wanted to catch to offer that kind of deal."

It *did* make me think. Maybe they were after a murderer, someone who had murdered prostitutes, and Caryn's black book held key evidence. It was totally plausible that someone wanting to cover up a previous murder, or murders, wouldn't have a problem killing the one person who could expose him.

Daisy left. I got ready for work and managed to come down the stairs into the chaos of school-day prep. Backpacks. Lunches. Henry had to take a hand-held game system back upstairs that he'd been trying to smuggle to school in his coat pocket. Madison had to go back upstairs to put on a shirt that didn't show half her midriff every time she raised her arm. I couldn't completely blame the girl for that one. She was tall and thin, and I was pretty sure any shirt she bought was going to be on the short side.

I grabbed my briefcase and eyed Judge Beck. "I'll take her shopping Sunday. We'll see if we can't find some longer shirts."

His shoulders slumped in relief. "Thanks. And if you're going to do that, then we'll go out to eat tonight instead of the sausage-noodle-casserole thing I was going to subject you to."

"Steak?" I asked hopefully.

He watched Madison stomp down the stairs, holding her arms up to display the coverage of her shirt. "Steak. And champagne. And dessert of your choice. If you're going to take her shopping, it's the least I can do."

Once at the office, I noticed that J.T. was looking rough this morning. His button-down shirt was rumpled, and both his bald head and chin were sporting some stubble. He looked up from his computer and gave me a wan smile. "A murderer in our town."

"Yeah." I wasn't sure what to say. We'd had overdoses, accidents, the rare drunk-driving accident that ended in fatality and a manslaughter charge. That was pretty much it. People didn't go around killing each other in Locust Point. It was something I hoped would never happen again.

"Here." I handed him the folder I'd taken home last night. "I did more research on Caryn Swanson. I think I found the dating site and listing she was using for the prostitution business. The police might be able to get more off of her computer or phone through her history."

"Thanks." J.T. took the folder and looked through it. "I spoke with the detective in charge of the investigation. They're going to search her house, but her car isn't there. I'm assuming she drove it and met someone somewhere and he dumped her body in that ditch as opposed to killing her there."

It made sense. And it also made me think. Where was her car? It had to be near, because I couldn't believe someone would risk driving a huge distance with a body in their car, or in Caryn's car. Was her purse and phone still in her car, or had the killer taken them?

"So, what's on my agenda today?" I had an idea I wanted to check out, but paying jobs came first.

"Two car repos I need you to track down for me, and another Creditcorp debtor."

I took the files from J.T. There went my morning, my afternoon, and probably my evening. But two car repos... Maybe I could check something else while I was tracking them down, and squeeze in a little time this afternoon to follow up if things worked out.

"I'll get right on these," I told J.T. "Think I can sneak out to MegaMart for a long lunch? If I'm not done by five, I'll finish up tonight from home."

J.T. shrugged. "Sure, go ahead. But if you're going to nose around that drainage pond, it's still roped off."

I shuddered at the thought. "No, just going to grab some baking supplies and a few other things."

And swing by the truck stop, but J.T. didn't have to know about that.

CHAPTER 16

*T*he Creditcorp job was involved, so I sat it aside for later and worked on the repos. I'm ashamed to admit that I always found these fun. Maybe J.T. wasn't alone in his love of drama and old fashioned investigative work, because automobile repossessions weren't the usual skip trace. These people knew someone was one tow truck away from snatching their car and went to all sorts of lengths to hide it. Sometimes it was at a friend's house. Sometimes it had swapped out license plates. Sometimes it had a new paint job and enough cosmetic modifications to render it virtually unrecognizable. All I could do was list the likely places, note down any traffic and parking tickets, then send J.T. out to look in windshields for VIN numbers.

It was close to three o'clock before I finished up the two repossessions and turned my attention to locating Caryn Swanson's car. I already had the registration from when she'd bought it, and a recent picture from a traffic camera confirmed the make, model, and license plate number. It was her only car, and there was no reason for her to switch plates, so I jotted down the information, gathered the Creditcorp paperwork for later, and locked the office for the day.

Against my better judgment, I drove to the back lot of the MegaMart to stare at the crime scene tape and replay the events from yesterday in my mind. This time there was no eerie shadow, no cold spots, no blue shoe, just a field of weeds leading down to a water-and-mud-filled ditch, all roped off with yellow streamers.

It gave me the creeps, so I drove back around front and parked there. By the time I left, I had enough flour, sugar, butter, chocolate, and spices to start an in-home bakery. I'd also grabbed dried fruit, fresh apples and oranges, and three zucchinis. I was so excited to revisit something I'd always enjoyed that I couldn't make up my mind which to make first. I foresaw a freezer full of muffins, cookies, and pies in my future as well as an increased waistline.

Once all the goods were in my car, I made the short jaunt on the overpass to the truck stop. Unlike the MegaMart, this place was open twenty-four-seven, and the parking lot here was always full. An abandoned car probably wouldn't be noticed for weeks, if not months. I drove up and down the lot, finally finding what I was looking for way in the back section where the huge trucks parked when the drivers wanted to snooze without being disturbed by patrons coming and going from the bar, the store, or the gas pumps.

There it was, a red late-model Mazda with tags that matched what was registered to Caryn Swanson. Just to make sure, I got out and looked through the windshield, comparing the VIN numbers. This was it. There was a layer of yellow pollen on the car that came from sitting still for more than a day in March when every tree within sight was blooming. Hanging from the rear-view mirror was a set of Mardi Gras beads. There was a cell phone charger plugged into the dash outlet. And there was a purse on the floor of the passenger side of the car, the strap peeking out from under the seat.

"That car's been here since the weekend." The man walking toward me had a green polo with a Hallvet Windows and Doors logo on it. His long poofy hair was pulled back into a ponytail, and he had a full beard reaching down several inches below his chin.

"Do you know when it got here and who was driving it?"

He shook his head. "Not sure. I came out Saturday night to play darts and saw it then. I don't usually park here, but I had my box truck from work that night."

"Do you think anyone else would have seen the owner?"

"Probably not. This is where the big rigs park. They pull in for six hours or so, then pull out. Whoever saw someone arrive in this car would be long gone."

I stared down through the windshield at the strap of the purse, then picked up my phone to call the police. Hopefully they'd find something here that would lead them to Caryn's killer.

"Weird place to park a car back here." The guy scratched his chin. "Mostly it's just truckers taking a nap, but sometimes a couple wanting to get busy will come back here. If you park behind a tractor-trailer, no one would see you from the road. They're all sleeping, so there's no bar traffic coming and going. Lighting is dim. If the couple keeps it quiet, no one would know."

I wondered if this was where Caryn Swanson had met her killer. I couldn't imagine a woman choosing a dimly lit, not well trafficked area to meet someone, but perhaps she did this so she'd not be seen, and not overheard. I guess with three or four truckers sleeping nearby, she'd have some confidence that they'd hear her scream and come to her aid if needed.

"Tons of condoms back there," the guy added. "The

truckers complain about it all the time, but the staff here never bothers to clean them up."

Eww. I wouldn't want to clean them up either. Ugh.

I thanked the window-and-door guy for his help and called in the location of the car. It felt somewhat anticlimactic, as though I was missing something important. There was just so much running around in my head right now. Was Caryn blackmailing a client? Was there some high-profile client, or someone who would lose big in a divorce—lose big enough to murder to protect their secret? Why would Caryn meet them here? And why in the world would she meet them at all?

CHAPTER 17

"*M*rs. Carrera?"

It was almost dinnertime. I was frantically trying to finish up the Creditcorp case before we headed out for steak, wanting to enjoy my dinner without this mess of a skip trace hanging over my head.

I looked up to see the girl who'd come home with Judge Beck and the kids, the same girl that had come home with them yesterday. I'd overheard something about a joint project, and this time the girls had stayed downstairs; poster board, books, and two laptops spread out on my dining room table.

"Yes, hon?" Honestly, I welcomed the interruption from my futile efforts to locate Richard Gibson.

She bit her lip, coming into the room. The girl had dark brown curls and a golden tan that clearly came from genetics rather than our anemic March sun. She was holding a folded piece of paper.

"I'm Chelsea Novak, Madison's friend. And…here."

I took the outstretched paper and unfolded it as Chelsea

shifted from foot to foot by my side. Sydney Vaughn. And a phone number. I looked up at the girl in confusion.

"Um, my sister Leah wanted me to give this to you." She looked nervously back toward the dining room and lowered her voice. "I'm in big trouble for going to that party. Leah is in worse trouble for taking me, but Sydney is her best friend and she's scared."

"Leah is scared? Or Sydney is scared?" And scared of what, having her cell phone taken away? Were their parents so strict that they'd be scared of a punishment?

"Sydney. She..." Chelsea looked to the dining room again, her voice practically a whisper. "Sydney was one of the girls. You know, the girls who did...stuff. For money."

In spite of the vague statements I was starting to connect the dots. "So, Sydney was one of the girls who worked for Caryn Swanson?"

Chelsea nodded.

"Did Leah work for Caryn Swanson?"

"No!" Chelsea looked horrified. "I mean, she was tempted because the money was really good but they guys all wanted weird stuff, and Leah thinks that's gross." She looked down at her hands and twisted them together. "Please don't tell anyone. Madison doesn't even know. Sydney is Leah's best friend and she'd never be allowed in our house again if my parents knew. And she doesn't want word to get out that she did these things."

I understood. This was the kind of thing that could follow a girl around for the rest of her life. Even if she left Locust Point, any future job in the public eye could dig up this scandal.

"So why tell me? What is Sydney afraid of?"

I was pretty sure she was afraid of meeting the same fate as her madam, but wanted Chelsea to tell me.

"I told Leah because she wanted to know how Judge and

Mrs. Beck found out about the party. After Caryn turned up dead, Sydney got scared. She doesn't want to go to the police because she doesn't want anyone to know what she did, but she says she knows things that might help find Caryn's killer."

No one knew who Caryn's prostitutes were. Sydney had good reason to keep it that way, and I'm sure none of the other girls wanted to be identified either. Besides the obvious fact that the murderer might kill again if he thought one of them knew his secret, nobody wanted to be known as a whore. Caryn Swanson had owned a successful party planning business. I was willing to bet a good number of her "girls" were from good families—well-connected families—and had jobs that might be in jeopardy if this came out.

"When should I call her?" I folded the paper and slid it under the Creditcorp file.

"Five in the morning. Sydney is in graduate school and she makes the rounds with the local large-animal veterinarian at six."

Ugh. I'd be up at that hour, but waking early to do yoga and eat muffins was a whole lot better than waking at five in the morning to go stick your arm up a cow's butt.

"Thanks," I told Chelsea. "And don't worry, I'll make every effort to keep your secrets."

I couldn't promise not to tell, not when a woman had been murdered, but if Sydney had something concrete she could give me, or somewhere I could point the police to, then I could hopefully keep both her and the Novak girls out of this.

Chelsea's mom picked her up soon after our chat, and Judge Beck hustled the children into the back seat of his sedan, leaving me to sit up front with him. It felt incredibly awkward, riding in a car with people I'd just met, up front with the judge while the kids in the back argued over which station to listen to.

Judge Beck finally put a stop to the argument by making an executive decision and putting on classical music. The kids groaned, and Henry made up silly lyrics to go along with Vivaldi. Madison laughed and joined in, and I realized that the judge had been right. She'd gotten over her sulk fairly quickly. I'm sure there would be moments of dark, silent-filled glares in the weeks to come, but overall, Madison seemed like a cheerful teenager. She hadn't needed prompting the last three days to do her homework, and although she was often glued to her phone, she put it aside and politely participated in conversation when addressed. I'd heard her at dinner with her brother and father, and got the impression she was intelligent, well-spoken, and fully able to hold her own against Henry's jibes and the judge's affectionate teasing.

But even so, I noticed that the shirt she'd changed into for dinner was quite a bit tighter and shorter than the one she'd been allowed to wear to school. I wasn't sure if the judge noticed, or if he was just picking his battles.

I'd expected us to pull into one of the chain restaurants near the big mall just outside of Milford, but Judge Beck drove into the downtown area, parallel parking on a side street where there was barely room for passing traffic to squeeze past the cars lining either side of the street.

Madison squealed. "Beurre Noisette? Dad, are we going to Beurre Noisette?"

The judge shot me a sheepish glance. "It's not as fancy as it sounds. The kids love their fries, and they *do* have good steaks."

Beurre Noisette was more of a traditional American steak house than a haven of French cuisine. The décor was a contemporary black and red with deco-style lighting and light jazz, but they served beer by the pitcher and the steaks were big enough to feed a third-world country. We squeezed into a booth, Henry on Judge Beck's side, and Madison on mine. Initially the girl was a bit reticent, but she made polite conversation with me, and by the time our crab dip had arrived, she was laughing and chatting away.

Both kids asked about my job, peppering me with questions about how I did my searches. Henry was particularly interested in the overgrown gardens behind my house, while Madison wanted to know if there were ghosts in my attic. I was amazed at what good conversationalists they were and decided I needed to compliment both Judge Beck and Heather on raising such well-mannered children who could carry on small talk better than most adults I knew.

Dinner was amazing. My steak was perfectly prepared, and my baked sweet potato had thick crystals of salt on the skin and a honey-cinnamon butter in the middle. The vegetable medley was crisp and full of flavor, and the triple chocolate cake we all shared would satisfy my sweet tooth for the rest of the week.

I hadn't had a dinner out like this since before Eli's accident, and as we ate, I struggled to keep the memories at bay. And failed. This wasn't the time for heartache, or thoughts of how much had been smashed within seconds that morning of the accident. Eli had loved eating out. There was an Ethiopian place near Stallworth that had been our favorite. If I closed my eyes, I could still see him scooping the food into the spongy buckwheat pancake. We'd fight over the potato stuff, arguing over whether we should get the chicken or the lamb. And after, we'd walk down the street arm-in-arm and look in the little galleries and antique shops that stretched the whole block. Sometimes we'd grab a gelato before heading home. And I'd rest my head on the car window, full and sleepy, watching the street lights go by, confident that Eli would bring us home safely. He'd reach his hand over, and we'd weave our fingers together, the only sound the swish of cars going the opposite way down the road.

"Track practice starts next week," Henry announced, jolting me from my reminiscence. "From three to six."

The fork froze halfway to Judge Beck's mouth. "Every day?"

The boy nodded. "Yeah for the first two weeks, then when we begin the meets, we're at practice Monday through Thursday."

Something lost and worn-down flitted across the judge's face, quickly hidden. "When are the meets?"

"Some weekday nights, some weekends. I have a copy of the schedule—one for you and one for Mom. The first two are at home, then three and four are away."

I saw the judge count on his fingers and realized he was trying to figure out which were his weekends. He had Monday through Thursday every other week, then alternating weekends right now.

"Where are the first two away games?"

Henry grabbed another forkful of cake. "Damascus and Eastlake. We have two more home meets after that, then a Thursday night at Milford that should be over at eight with Saturday at Washdale High."

The lost look remained a little longer this time. "What time are the meets?"

The boy shrugged. "Depends. Most start at seven or eight in the morning and go until five. Longer once we get to the county and state competitions."

Madison was watching her father intently. "Softball starts the week after, but I don't think I'm going to play this year."

"No, you're doing softball." Judge Beck shook his head, like he was trying to clear his thoughts. "You love softball and your coach thinks you might wind up with a scholarship if you keep playing like you did last season. You're not giving up softball."

"But my practices will be from five to eight, after the baseball team practice," Madison pointed out.

The judge winced. "You're not giving up softball. We'll just have to work around the schedules."

I could practically read his thoughts. Drop the kids off at school. Pick one up, then go back for the other later and figure out how to work dinner into the equation. Homework. Conflicting home and away meets and games on the weekends. And I'd seen the work Judge Beck brought home with him each night. How late was he up in his bedroom working, papers spread everywhere?

For a brief moment, I was relieved I hadn't had to go through this. And as much as I was tempted to jump in and offer to help him out, this wasn't my family, and it wasn't my problem. If he was going to be a single dad with half custody, he was going to have to figure it out. Women did it all the time, and I'll admit I felt a bit of vindication for my gender watching him struggle over the very logistical issues women everywhere dealt with on a daily basis.

"Are we still going shopping Sunday?" Madison asked. "It's Mom's weekend, but she said you could take me."

"Mrs. Kay offered to go with you."

I saw a flash of disappointment in the girl's face before her expression composed into one of bland neutrality. It reminded me so much of her father. "That's all right. We'll do it some other time."

It wasn't his weekend? I'd forgotten, and just assumed I'd be filling in for an hour or two while he did something with Henry. I couldn't imagine Heather giving up even a few hours of her weekend, which meant Madison must have asked to have her father take her. And he'd shuffled that task over to me. What a jerk. I knew guys were sometimes clueless about this sort of thing, but it had to have hurt Madison terribly.

I pulled back my foot and let it fly, kicking the judge hard in the shin. He jumped, giving me a "what-the-heck" look.

Shopping, I mouthed, jerking my head toward Madison.

His what-the-heck look changed to one of horror. I knew spending two hours with a teenage girl looking at makeup and t-shirts was probably close to being drawn and quartered, but this was his daughter. I glared at him, once again jerking my head toward Madison.

"Oh, no, honey, I'll take you," he announced. It sounded the same way someone might say "I love eating pickled herring" or "no, that dress doesn't make you look fat at all." "I'll take you. I just thought maybe you would prefer... someone else. Like someone who's a woman."

Madison gave him that raised eyebrow look. "You don't want to do it. You don't want to go."

"No, I *do* want to go. I really do. I can't wait to go."

Okay, that was going a bit too far. Madison must have realized it, too. Her lips twitched and she hid the smile behind a napkin. "Good. It'll be fun. There are some new stores I want to go to, and Nicole says that Total Tart has some really cute skirts they just got in. I want to check out the eyeshadows at Beauty Station, too, and maybe look at some purses if we have time."

Judge Beck's eyes glazed over. He glanced at me, desperation on his face. *Look elsewhere, buddy. I'm not saving you.*

The rest of dessert was spent discussing which electives the kids wanted to take in the fall, and where they wanted to go for summer vacation. I got peppered with questions about what Taco liked to eat, about the house across the street with the washing machines and broken lawnmowers in the yard, and if I planned on getting the hot tub up and working sometime soon.

By the time we got home, I was full and happy. I hadn't felt this happy in a long time. Every now and then I'd see a bluebird at the feeder, or feel Taco's purr under my hand, or wake up warm and snug in my bed and feel a contented sort of happy, but this was different. This felt like my cup was brimming over. It felt like maybe I needed to go shopping and buy a bigger cup. Like maybe a giant soup-bowl sized mug, or one of those never-enough-coffee type mugs.

The kids went up for their bedtime routine and I headed to the kitchen, pulling out recipes for muffins, pies, and zucchini bread. There wouldn't be time to make anything tonight, but I could pick out a recipe, make sure I had the ingredients, then spend a lovely evening tomorrow baking something yummy.

Orange spice muffins. Yes, that was it. They'd be perfect for a cool March post-yoga breakfast. Maybe I'd grab a bottle of champagne and squeeze some oranges, and Daisy and I would indulge a bit. I chuckled, thinking what Judge Beck would say to see us drinking mimosas at six in the morning. Wine on the porch with Daisy the first day he'd come by. Wine the evening after I'd discovered Caryn Swanson's body. Booze after yoga. He was going to think I was a total lush.

Well, what use was it being a sixty-year-old widow if I couldn't be allowed some eccentricities? Still amused and thinking of other new and outrageous things I might want to start making part of my daily routine, I went to the study and packed up my files for tomorrow.

And there was the note with Sydney Vaughn's phone number. I unfolded it, smoothing the crease as I climbed the stairs to my bedroom. I might as well have this right by my bedside so I didn't forget to call the one person who might have a clue as to who the murderer was in our midst.

CHAPTER 18

*F*ive in the morning came far too soon. I brushed my teeth, splashed some water on my face, and hoped I'd be coherent enough to speak with Sydney Vaughn pre-coffee. I might have felt like my brain was stuffed with cotton, but the woman on the other end of the phone line was wide awake and chipper.

At least she was chipper until I told her who I was.

"I don't want the police to know anything," she told me in a low voice. "Illegality aside, it would kill my parents to know what I was doing. No one in this town would ever let me forget it. And aside from that, I don't want to have that sicko come after me. He's already killed Caryn. I'm sure he wouldn't think twice about killing me, too."

Her voice choked on the last two sentences, and I remembered Chelsea say that Caryn and Sydney had been friends.

"How did you get started in this? And what was the process?"

"I met Caryn through some mutual friends. We were talking one night and I was complaining about the cost of grad school and how I'd be paying student loans until I was sixty. She said I could make good money as an "escort." I was interested and when we spoke later, she said there was a whole lot more money if I would have sex with the guys. It was totally discrete, all cash through Caryn, so nothing changed hands with me. She'd message me and describe the client, and if I was interested, she'd set it up."

Sounded like pretty straightforward, high-end prostitution. Not something to kill someone over.

"After a few months, she told me a few clients were kinky. She'd tell me what they liked, and if I agreed to it, the pay was huge. It was some weird stuff, but nothing harmful to me."

I didn't want to know, but I knew I had to ask. "What type of kinky stuff?"

"Not tying up or spanking or stuff like that. Mostly guys who want to slobber all over your feet, or have you pretend that they're babies, or pee on them. Like I said, weird stuff, but nothing where I'd be scared or feel like I was in danger. They were nice guys. And like I said, the money was good."

Would someone kill over the possibility of being exposed as liking this sort of stuff? Maybe if they were a school teacher, or a corporate CEO, or a politician. "Did you know these clients? I mean, were they local? Did they give you names or phone numbers?"

"Caryn had all that. I called them by a fake name. And they weren't local. I remember one guy saying he drove two hours to meet me. That's how private these guys wanted to keep this. It's not like I wanted anyone to know about it either. That's why Caryn picked the girls she did. The clients could be confident that we weren't about to blackmail them or reveal their secrets, even if we found out who they were. We had just as much to lose as they did."

"But if Caryn was about to turn over her client list, her

black book, maybe someone decided they had too much too lose?"

"She wasn't going to turn it over. They didn't have anything on her that would stick, and she was determined to ride it out."

"But someone didn't know that," I countered.

"They…that's who she was meeting Friday night. She'd gotten out of jail and said she needed to meet a client—a special client that she'd been providing for on her own. She wanted to reassure him that she wasn't going to expose him."

"Was she blackmailing him?" I could see no other reason for this guy to kill her, unless he didn't believe that she was going to hold out.

"No! She didn't need to blackmail him. This guy paid really well. Like really, really well. Caryn had enough cash set aside to buy a house. She couldn't deposit it all because the banks report large deposits, so she was stockpiling cash until she figured out a way to get it through the system and make it legitimate. But the last few times I saw her, she was worried. This guy liked intense stuff and it had reached the point where Caryn was getting scared. But what could she do?"

"She could stop seeing him. Tell him the deal was off and he'd need to go elsewhere."

"She couldn't. There was the money, but she said was worried if she cut him off, he'd make things hard for her, mess up her business. She told me that she'd found out that he'd killed a girl a long time ago. He said it was an accident. But while she wasn't worried he'd do that to her, it still bothered her."

Well, yeah. Providing sex to a guy who had murdered a girl "a long time ago" would bother any sane woman. The insane part was that she continued to do it. "And she didn't go to the police?"

"And say what? A john might ruin her business unless she let him choke her during sex? That he'd said he'd accidently killed someone, but she had no idea who or when? Caryn said the guy had connections and money. No one would believe her. Even if it went to trial, he'd probably be acquitted. When she went missing, I thought maybe she went into hiding, but after I heard they found her dead, I knew this guy killed her."

Choke her? I'll admit I'm not particularly prudish and I'd managed to hear about all sorts of strange things consenting adults did, but choking? How could that possibly be fun, either on the giving or the receiving end? "You said she was supposed to meet him?"

"Yeah. Friday night. She was going to reassure him that she wasn't going to turn over the client list or turn him in. She thought that as long as he knew she wouldn't expose him, then he'd be okay, and he'd probably go somewhere else for his kink since she had the police on her tail."

It made sense. But if this client hadn't killed Caryn, who had? A different client that wasn't reassured she was going to keep her mouth shut? A jealous wife?

"I have the book."

"What?" I couldn't have heard Sydney right.

"It was in my post box yesterday morning. Caryn must have put it in the mail Friday before she went to meet that guy." Sydney's voice broke on a sob. "Oh, God. She must have known he might do something. She must have known."

"Sydney, you have to give that book to the police," I urged her. "They're looking for it. Caryn was murdered, and that book might have the killer's name."

"I can't. I don't want anyone to know what I did. Caryn was my friend, and I want her murderer to rot in jail for the rest of his life, but I don't want my life ruined. And I don't want him coming after me."

"Can you give it to the police anonymously? Mail it to them?"

She sniffed. "I'll bring it to you. I don't want it to get lost in the mail, but I can't take it in myself. Just tell them you found it. You're an investigator, say you discovered it somewhere."

I was a skip tracer, not an investigator, but it didn't matter enough to correct Sydney. "I'm leaving for work at eight. Can you get it here before then? Or I can meet you."

"No, I don't want to be seen meeting you either. And I'll be out on calls until afternoon. Can I just bring it by your house? Do you have somewhere I can put it?"

I was going to have an ulcer worrying all afternoon that it had gotten stolen, or rained on, or chewed by a roaming neighborhood dog. But if this was the only way to get the book, I'd have to deal. "There's a grill in the back yard. The gate is unlocked. Just stick it in the grill."

I'd need to make sure there weren't any wasp nests in the grill before I went to work, and put down some foil so the book didn't get charcoal dust on it.

I gave Sydney my address and my phone number, telling her to call me if there were any problems or if she needed to talk again. Then I hung up, threw on my clothes, and ran downstairs to make coffee before morning yoga with Daisy.

CHAPTER 19

J.T. was out delivering the Creditcorp files that I'd finally managed to complete, leaving me with background checks on three of his potential bail clients. Normally he didn't go to this length on petty theft and felony possession, but having Caryn Swanson vanish for a few days made him extra cautious. I watched the clock, eager to get back home and check inside my grill for the black book.

Finally, I could take it no longer and ran home around one o'clock. I'd whacked out three, thankfully empty, wasp nests from the cooker, then carefully covered both the grill and the inside of the lid so the evidence wouldn't have greasy black marks all over it. When I lifted the lid, I breathed out in relief to see a leather-bound book, the type people use for journaling, inside. I paged through it briefly, Taco yowling at my feet for attention. Caryn seemed to have written her notes in some kind of code. I was pretty sure it didn't rise to the level of military intelligence, so figured with a few hours of work I might be able to decode enough of it to hopefully point me in the right direction. Then, I'd need to find a way to get it to the police without implicating Sydney or coming across as a total idiot. Or a person of interest. I'd found the body. I'd found Caryn's car. Now I amazingly "found" the black book?

Once I got back to the office, I got to work, copying down the numbers and initials and the number of times they were repeated. Whoever choking-guy was, he was clearly a regular and the most likely suspect. I wasn't completely ruling out other regular clients, but I figured he'd be one of the ones with the most entries. Luckily for all her code work, Caryn seemed to use a standard date and time format to account for the scheduled meetings. I marked up a calendar with the codes, then stood back to see what I had.

I was guessing the first set of letters and numbers represented the client. The second set was the service provider. Then the two sets of numbers following were the amount the client paid, then the amount due to the provider. The last set, from what I could tell, indicated what, if any, the kink was to be.

There were a lot of repeats, but only one happened all year long, and that one had a single payment number, which had to mean Caryn herself was taking care of that client. BBR5. I'd need to figure out who that was since CS1 stood for Caryn. The payments were high in the beginning, but as time went on, they got astoundingly large. And the set of letters and numbers sometimes repeated but more often changed. The last twenty entries were BP, the early ones labeled as a 1 and the last few as a 3. Was that the amount of times or the length or something to indicate the intensity? Given that Sydney had said this guy liked to choke his partners, I was assuming BP was breath play.

Ugh. I was going to need to shower in Lysol after this was all over. I sorted all the kinks and quickly discovered that this BBR5, unlike the others, seemed to be pretty much straight sex until the breath play commenced. I was no expert, but I would have assumed autoerotic asphyxiation would come after a progressively intense pattern of BDSM, not this. It seemed that this guy's only kink interest was the breath play.

But why would that be something that would have gotten Caryn killed? It didn't seem nearly as off-putting as having someone pee on you, but there was a kind of psycho, serial killer vibe to it. I hated to judge, but as much as I wouldn't want a school teacher who was into rubber nun suits, one that enjoyed choking their sexual partners would be a job-ending revelation. It would be a job-ending revelation for most all careers.

I read the book cover to cover and found nothing to indicate who BBR5 could be. There had to be something more. Maybe Caryn's cell phone had a listing that could be traced, or her e-mails would provide some indication of who this was. Either way, I didn't have the resources to get that information. It was time to call the police.

First, I called J.T., who came straight back to the office, amazed that someone would have left such a valuable piece of evidence on our doorstep while I was out at lunch. Why us? Why not the police or Caryn's lawyer? I shrugged, and slapped on my best poker face, trying to appear innocent. He glanced through the book, then handed it over to the detective that had come by. We answered questions, and I began to pack up my files for more evening at-home work. Just as the detective was leaving, Pete Briscane came through the door. He blinked in surprise to see the officer, then they exchanged some polite conversation while I stalled, pretending to look through a file cabinet.

"Pete!" J.T. walked over and shook the mayor's hand, slapping him on the shoulder. "Sushi or that new Italian place in Milford?"

Ah. I knew they were friends, and that Pete had confided in J.T. some issue with his son. Guess tonight's dinner would be part two of the man's family troubles. Poor guy.

"Italian. I've been dying to try that place. Donna is gluten-free, so we never get to go." He looked out the window at the detective getting into his car. "You found the black book? Weird that it would have turned up here."

"Kay found it on the doorstep when she got back from lunch. I'm assuming one of Caryn Swanson's girls had it but was too afraid of implicating herself to turn it in."

The mayor looked over at me, his blue eyes twinkling. "Did you look through it? I know, I know, I'm just as much of a gossip as everyone else in this town. We've never had a prostitution ring bust before, and I can't recall the last murder. I'm curious who her clients were."

I smiled back, stuffing a few extra folders into my bag that I wouldn't need. "I'll admit I did read it. It was mostly in code though—letters and numbers. I'm sure the police will figure it out."

He sighed. "I hope so. Then we can all go back to normal and worry about things like who is going to race in this year's regatta. You're sponsoring a boat, aren't you, J.T.?"

My boss rolled his eyes. "I'm sure you'll talk me into it eventually. Let's go. Kay, will you lock up?"

I nodded and watched the two men leave, still teasing each other over the regatta. Pete Briscane was such a nice guy. Too bad he had such a reprobate for a son. I looked down at the sticky note attached to a file folder with David Briscane's name on it. Tonight's work should wrap up fairly quickly. If I had a chance, maybe I'd dig into David's background a bit more. Because the mayor wasn't the only nosy, gossipy one in this town.

CHAPTER 20

J took a break from work, baking up muffins and a pie while eating salad and listening to classic rock. The house was oddly quiet. Funny how after decades of just Eli and mefollowed by a month of me and a cat, I'd quickly gotten used to a roommate and two teenagers. In three days, I'd come to love the bustle and the coming and going of the three additions to my home. But tonight, the kids were with their mother, and from Judge Beck's absence, I guessed he'd taken advantage of that fact to catch up on some work.

Which is what I intended to do myself. Leaving the pie out to cool, safeguarded from the cat by an elaborate ring of wire racks and cookie sheets, I grabbed one of the muffins, fixed a pot of tea, and headed into my study. By eight o'clock, I'd finished the two background checks for the bail customers, and was just beginning to pull up a case search on David Briscane when the judge came through the front door.

"There's muffins in the kitchen," I called out. "Don't eat the pie. It's for tomorrow night."

He poked his head in. "I won't say no to a muffin, and I'll

be sure to be home early tomorrow if there's pie in the plans."

"Apple spice with a cheddar cheese crust," I told him. "I'm going to cook that chicken I'm thawing in the fridge, too. You're welcome to leftovers if you end up working late again."

He came into the room, rubbing his eyes with one hand. "Thanks. I feel guilty sponging dinner off you, but I'm so far behind on these briefs. Picking the kids up from school, getting them dinner, and getting them to school the next morning takes a bite out of my workday. I never appreciated how much time parenting takes. Heather always did all of this, where my role was just to work and bring in the money to support the four of us. Juggling both a job and the kids is more difficult than I thought."

"Change is hard. You'll get a routine down soon enough. And it won't all be shopping for purses and makeup with your teenage daughter."

He grimaced, half-sitting on the edge of my desk. "I hope not. Her softball games are fun, but I hope this purse-and-makeup phase goes away soon."

"Don't count on it," I teased, turning back to my computer screen.

Judge Beck followed my gaze, scowling as he saw the case search I'd pulled up. "You're checking on David Briscane?"

I nodded. "Just being nosy. J.T. said he was in town to meet with his father last weekend. I know he'd been in a bunch of trouble as a kid and wondered if he'd shaped up or not."

The judge's frown deepened. "He had got in some *serious* trouble as a kid. I'm surprised he's not in jail, honestly."

I looked up in surprise. "For a DWI and drugs? Was he that much of a user in high school?"

"No, actually, he was clean as far as drugs and alcohol

back then. In high school, he wasn't really a problem beyond a few pranks like turning the water in the City Hall fountain green, or putting tuna fish in mailboxes one summer until this serious thing happened. I wasn't involved since the case was moved elsewhere, but I heard about it through the grapevine."

What other trouble? And what trouble could be bad enough to send David Briscane to court, and have the case moved out of the county?

"He was a minor?" Nothing had come up on a case search. That plus the judge's reticence in naming the "issue" meant that David Briscane must have been under eighteen when it happened.

Judge Beck nodded. "Yeah, just under eighteen."

He wasn't tried as an adult, so it couldn't have been *that* bad. I ran through possible scenarios in my mind and came up with involuntary manslaughter. That's the sort of thing that wouldn't be pushed into an adult trial, and depending on the evidence, might even result in probation before judgment. And I could see Mayor Briscane, then Councilman Briscane, wanting to have the trial moved out of the county away from prying eyes and wagging tongues.

I looked back at the screen, at the minor charges listed over the last five years for David Briscane. "Well, whatever it was, he must have learned his lesson, because none of this looks any worse than half of the young men in town."

Judge Beck stood, giving the computer screen one last glance. "I hope so, because I really don't want to see that come up on the docket ever again."

CHAPTER 21

"*H*ey Daisy, do you remember David Briscane, the mayor's son?" We were relaxing in the back-yard gazebo with our coffee and the freshly made muffins from last night. This morning's temperature was close to sixty and I found myself looking around the yard, planning where some spring bulbs might look nice. It would be too late for them to bloom this year, but if I got some in now, next spring would be gorgeous.

She nodded. "Yeah. Is he back in town? His father basically forbade him to come within a hundred miles of Locust Point."

No wonder if he'd been in as much trouble as Judge Beck had implied. "He was meeting with his Dad last weekend. I'm assuming he probably needs money."

Daisy sniffed. "I doubt it. After what happened in high school, his parents gave him a huge sum in trust. I'm talking huge. Then they sent him away to college and set him up in business on the other side of the state. I've got no idea why Pete would even agree to see him."

My curiosity was killing me. "What happened in high

school? A manslaughter case? Reckless driving? A dare gone wrong?"

"Hardly. He strangled a girl." Daisy's voice was tight. "It was a teenage girl from Milford. Pete hushed it all up because he didn't want a scandal. The girl was poor, and David had the best lawyers, so he got probation. It's all sealed and off his record since he was a minor at the time."

I was in so much shock that I could barely think. "Strangled? He *strangled* a girl to death and got *probation*? What on God's green earth is going on with our judicial system?"

And the parallels to Caryn Swanson's client weren't escaping me. Could the killer possibly be the mayor's son?

Daisy shot me a grim look. "He said it was some sex thing gone wrong, that it was consensual and they'd just taken it too far. Evidently, they'd done it before. Her friends testified that the girl liked that kind of thing. So it wound up being ruled an accident. A tragic, kinky accident."

I just couldn't imagine this. "Was it? I mean, how do you know this, when no one else in town does?"

"I knew the girl. We had an outreach thing going on and she was one of my kids. She wasn't kinky. I don't believe she liked that sort of thing. But she was poor, and desperate, and from what I could tell, he was giving her money to participate. I didn't know who it was or what was happening, or I would have gone straight to Pete myself. I knew she was having sex with someone, knew she was getting paid. I saw some bruises on her neck, and thought maybe she was being beaten up either by this boyfriend or someone at home. I was trying to help her, but with abuse victims, it takes time. I didn't have time. She didn't, either. She was dead before I could get her to leave him."

Oh, poor Daisy. Poor...Milford girl. "What was her name?" She needed a name. She couldn't be some nameless girl strangled ten years ago.

"Desiree Trottenhaus."

Poor Desiree Trottenhaus.

Strangled. Just like Caryn Swanson had been strangled. Just like some john had paid a whole lot of money to have Caryn participate in this sort of thing. And David Briscane had been back in town that weekend. Had he killed Caryn to avoid having all that brought up again? Had he killed her, then gone to Pete for help, or had he asked Pete for help, then killed Caryn because he'd been turned down?

But I had no proof. There was nothing beyond some obscure code in a black book and the word of a woman who would refuse to testify that Caryn had a client who liked that sort of thing. Even so, there had to be more than one person in the state who had that kink. David Briscane could claim it had been a teenage thing and that he'd given that up after he'd accidently killed his partner. There was no proof. None at all.

Daisy headed home and I purposely stayed in the kitchen, waiting to ambush Judge Beck when he came down. As soon as he walked into the kitchen, I handed him a cup of coffee and went right for the jugular.

"I know David Briscane was tried for involuntary manslaughter for strangling that girl from Milford in some sex game gone wrong. What's your thought on it? Is he the type who would do it again? Was it just teenage experimentation, or something he truly enjoys?"

Judge Beck sipped his coffee and slowly shook his head. "You're like a terrier, Kay. You just dig and dig and dig. I've got no idea how you discovered that between last night and this morning, but I'm thinking Pierson isn't paying you enough."

True, but that didn't answer my question. "I've got reason to believe one of Caryn Swanson's clients, one she serviced personally, was into breath play. What are the odds that David Briscane might be that client?"

The judge frowned thoughtfully. "His father pretty much banned him from the town. I can't imagine David would risk coming here just to pay someone for sex."

"But sex that involved strangulation? I'm willing to bet most prostitutes wouldn't touch that one no matter the money. Caryn Swanson was running a ring that catered to all sorts of kinks that people wouldn't want publicly known. Guys drove hours to come here and get...stuff that they couldn't get elsewhere."

"I guess. But I'm not sure..." He took another drink of coffee. "David confessed. He knew things that only the one who killed that girl would know. Her friends said it had been consensual, that they had been together for quite a few months. But there's been nothing since then. Either it was teen experimentation and he never did it again, or he perfected his technique and hasn't pushed it too far."

"David was paying that girl. And Caryn's client didn't kill her in a sex act. I think he killed her because he was worried she'd expose him to get a lesser sentence."

The judge frowned. "Possibly. I don't know. I think it's someone else. I got a weird vibe during that whole thing with David. I wasn't a judge then, and I didn't have anything to do with the trial, but I knew people who did. He just didn't seem like the killer type. He seemed like a scared kid who was willing to confess and take whatever the justice system dealt him. I think that's one of the reasons he got a PBJ. He came across as horrified over the whole thing and completely accepting the fact that he might go to jail. He was penitent."

Maybe I was going down the wrong road. I trusted Judge Beck's opinion, trusted that he had good intuition on these sorts of things. From what he'd said, David didn't sound like the type who would be a repeat offender. He might have been a troublemaker, and continued to have some minor run-ins with the law, but nothing that would indicate he was continuing this sort of sexual activity, let alone be capable of premeditated murder.

"There was that one witness," he mused. "Someone who claimed she knew the victim from some community action program and said that David wasn't the one who killed the girl. He confessed, and all the other evidence pointed to him, so the prosecution just assumed she was a nutcase or a druggie and didn't pursue it. Sheila something. Not that it mattered."

It probably didn't matter. David Briscane killed that girl back in high school, and I felt that he was probably the top suspect in Caryn Swanson's murder, too. "I know you don't believe me, but he was in town during the window that Caryn Swanson was most likely killed, he had the same kink as one of her personal clients. And with a PBJ, he most definitely wouldn't want to be exposed as continuing to strangle his sexual partners."

Judge Beck shook his head. "It doesn't add up, Kay. His being here and the similarity in the kink is circumstantial. We've no idea if that client is the one that killed Swanson, and David would have no reason to kill her even if he were the client. Autoerotic asphyxiation between consensual partners isn't a crime. It's not like he'd suffer if his reputation was damaged. Anyone who did some digging could undercover the previous trial, which you just proved. He owns a barbeque joint on the other side of the state. He was a minor and it was involuntary manslaughter. Why kill a woman over being exposed as someone who paid for kinky sex?"

He was right, but outside of the motivation, there were too many coincidences for me to ignore. There had to be something down this road. Whether it led to David Briscane or not, I had to keep going down it.

CHAPTER 22

J had a stack of files awaiting me at work, which was surprising for a Friday. Four skip traces for a new client that we wanted to impress with a thorough investigation and a quick turn-around, two bail clients to research, and one boat repossession. How someone expected to hide a boat was beyond me. We wouldn't be able to go into a garage to retrieve it, but it would be easy enough to get a court order while making sure the debtor didn't hook it up to a truck and haul it away.

J.T. came in around ten, looking stressed. His formerly bald head was sporting some fuzz, and the grungy jeans-and-tank-top look was back, paired with a set of cowboy boots. I gave him the work I'd done yesterday and reviewed it with him, jotting down the priorities for today and telling him I'd take home anything I didn't get done today. I was working as much in the evening as Judge Beck lately. I liked being busy and I loved my job, but the last few days had been too busy for me to immerse myself in a baking extravaganza or try to master the art of the knitted washcloth. Plus, I still had the rest of Eli's stuff to go through, the herb garden to replant, and the hot tub to prep and fill for the kids. And Taco had been sadly neglected the last two days. The cat clearly needed more petting, and my evening hours at the computer weren't allowing me to have much kitty-time. Maybe I should ask for a raise.

"Hey, what do you know about David Briscane's legal troubles?" I asked him once we were done with the review of the day's work.

His eyebrows shot up. "He did some vandalism of the City Hall fountain like ten years ago. Mostly just kids-gone-wild kind of stuff. I know Pete was really stressed about his shenanigans and was worried that David's actions would reflect badly on him and ruin his political career. Then when that scandal happened David's senior year, I thought Pete was going to wind up with a heart attack."

"The manslaughter case," I commented.

J. T. nodded, but shot me a surprised look. "Pete covered that up pretty well. It was in Milford. The two were minors. The trial got moved three counties away. Even as bad as gossip is in this town, I doubt more than a handful of people knew about it. And those who did felt sorry for Pete. No one wanted to see him ruined because his son screwed up and accidently killed some girl."

That was a pretty big screw up. I couldn't help but bristle at J.T.'s dismissal of the fact that a girl *died*. "Do you think it was just youthful sexual experimentation, or that David is really into that sort of thing, that he might still be into that sort of thing?"

"You don't think..." His eyes widened. "Do you think David was one of Caryn Swanson's clients? But why? Why would he drive hours to get sex? He's a good-looking guy, and a charge as a minor wouldn't keep him from getting any bootie."

"She specialized in kink, and that was one of the kinks she provided."

J.T.'s gaze slid over to my computer screen. "You found all that out online? Good grief, our detectives need to start doing this. They could solve cases without leaving the station."

I figured I'd just let him believe that. No sense in going into a long explanation about Daisy's volunteer work years ago and Sydney's side job. "Caryn Swanson provided that kind of service. Many of their clients drove a considerable distance for this sort of thing. If David was into it, maybe he was one of her clients. Maybe he really didn't want anyone, especially his father, to find out."

It was a weak motive and I knew it, but J.T. nodded. "I should tell Pete. He'll blow a gasket. David has been so much trouble. This time, he'll probably just let him go to jail. A man can't be held to blame for his son's behavior, especially when he's done so much to help him."

For some weird reason, I didn't want Pete to know. Was it that I didn't want him thinking I was a snoop? That I was afraid that I was wrong as Judge Beck said, and I'd be causing an innocent man grief? Or because I was afraid that I was right and I'd wind up with a target on my head?

"It's a theory," I hastily explained. "Probably a bit of a stretch. I mean, I'm not a detective, and I'm not privy to the details of the case."

"Still, I should let Pete know. I mean, if this woman provided that kind of sex, it's a possibility that David is in that black book we gave to the police."

"Do you think he still does that sort of thing?" I asked, returning to my original question. "Maybe it's a coincidence and what he did was just a one-time thing that went wrong."

J.T. thought for a moment. "He's weird. I hate to say that about Pete's son, but he's weird. Nervous and jumpy, kind of sullen. I think if he did that once, he was most likely into that sort of thing. Kids experiment, but not with *that*. It takes a sick mind to do that sort of thing."

It still didn't explain the lack of concrete motive. David might be weird and he still might enjoy strangling women as a part of sex, but he didn't have anything to lose in having that kink exposed.

J.T. left for the day and I worked on the stack of files beside my computer. Around lunch time, I called Daisy and asked her if she'd ever known a Sheila, who was Desiree Trottenhaus's friend.

"She wasn't really a friend; she was someone who was in the program with Desiree. Why?"

"I heard that she didn't think David Briscane killed Desiree, that the boyfriend who was paying her to have sex was someone else."

Daisy sucked in a breath. "Then why would David take the fall for it? He confessed."

"Sometimes innocent people confess and plead guilty when they feel the evidence is so overwhelming that they'll never appear innocent to a jury." I thought again about what Judge Beck had said. If David had been covering for someone, he had to have known the details that only the killer knew. Was it a friend? Was it a lover? Maybe David was gay and his bisexual lover killed the girl by accident, and David took the fall, knowing his Dad would get him the best lawyers and help him with the trial.

Maybe I was really, really stretching. David knew the details. He'd confessed and thrown himself on the mercy of the court. This Sheila must have been confused. Maybe Desiree was getting paid for sex by multiple men. Maybe David had nothing at all to do with Caryn Swanson or her death.

"Sheila Pitt. I can look her up and see what happened to

her. She used to live in Bradley Heights, just outside of Milford."

I thanked Daisy and asked her to text me if she found anything. Then I hung up and got to work. By quitting time, I still had a stack of folders I'd need to take home with me, but I had Sheila Pitt's phone number. I left a message for her, explaining the reason for my call, then packed up and headed for home.

A small white envelope fluttered out from the crack in the door to the ground as I walked out. I picked it up and carefully opened it. Sometimes clients dropped by checks for payment of various services, and left them in the door. I was pretty sure I would have heard someone knock, but maybe I'd been too engrossed in my research to notice.

I know who killed Caryn Swanson. I'm afraid to go to the police. Meet me back behind the truck stop where the semis park at ten tonight.

The same spot where I'd found Caryn's car. I might be a terrier, as Judge Beck called me, but I wasn't stupid. There was no way I was going to go traipsing around a dimly-lit section of the truck stop parking area with heavily sleeping truckers. Still, I was very curious as to who this was. It could be legitimate, or it could be a trap. Well, I intended to set a trap of my own. If this was one of Caryn's girls who wanted to come forward, I'd follow up. If it was the killer, then the police would follow up.

CHAPTER 23

I was home finishing up the case files from today with Taco snoozing on my lap and the remains of my chicken dinner perched precariously at the edge of my desk. The sun had long dipped below the horizon, moonlight peeking through the window. Judge Beck still wasn't home. I doubted he was out with friends or on a date with the divorce in process.

My phone rang. And I recognized the number. Sheila. I answered and waited for her to respond.

"You're an investigator? Looking into a death in Locust Point?"

"Yes." Sort of. "I was told you had information on a case years ago—Desiree Trottenhaus. She died during a sex act and David Briscane confessed to the crime?"

"He didn't do it, and it wasn't a sex act gone wrong. I mean, yes, Desiree was having sex for money, and that was a part of the deal with one particular guy, but it wasn't that David. And it wasn't an accident. This guy knew what he was doing. He killed her on purpose."

"Wait, how do you know it wasn't David?"

Sheila sniffed. "Because Desiree did it for money, and kids don't have money. And she told me this guy was old, like her dad's age. It was kinda gross, but he paid a lot. The strangling thing started out with him just holding her neck. Then it got tighter and tighter each time until she'd almost pass out. She said it was a real rush. She liked it."

None of this was making sense. "So why would he kill her if she liked it, if she was a willing participant?"

"Because she was sixteen, and she wasn't very good at keeping her mouth shut. It's one thing to do kinky stuff with a boy a year older than you; it's another to do it with an adult man."

It wasn't just that this was an unsavory kink, it was with a minor. This guy had a lot to lose if this came out, and if Caryn Swanson turned over the black book and he was discovered, someone was going to connect the dots.

David Briscane was innocent. And there was only one person I could think of who he'd take the fall for, someone who had some power and influence over him, someone who could throw his weight around and get him probation for involuntary manslaughter, someone who could give him a whole lot of money as opposed to throwing him out of the house. And as a minor, he wouldn't even carry a record if he was convicted.

"Would you testify on this? Go to the police?"

She snorted. "Of course. I went to the police before, but no one wanted to believe a teenager from the 'hood. I'm not afraid of this guy, and I want to see Desiree's real killer put away."

Good, because I had every intention of seeing that, too. I thanked Sheila and told her I'd be in touch, then got in my car to drive out to the truck stop.

Trip. That was the guy's name who played darts and

drove a box truck delivering doors and windows. He grinned when he saw me, extending a set of darts.

"Wanna play? Winner buys the next round."

"Actually, I wondered if you'd do a job for me. A little surveillance."

Trip sat the darts down and picked up his beer. "Like camping outside some woman's house and taking pictures of her having sex with the gardener?"

"No, hanging out where the overnight parking is, where the truckers sleep and that car was. Somebody is going to come there tonight, someone who isn't a trucker. I want you to take pictures of him, note when he's there, when he leaves, what he does."

Trip gave me a thumbs-up. "How much?"

I didn't have much and I had no idea how much this sort of thing cost, so I quickly calculated the cost of half a dozen beers and a decent rib eye and quoted that.

He nodded. "Sounds good. There's no one to play darts with tonight anyway. Well, no one who isn't plowed out of their mind from happy hour."

I gave Trip my cell phone number and asked him to text me the details and the pictures tonight, no matter how late. Then I gave him half the money and promised him the other half once I'd gotten everything. He headed out to the back where four semis were parked. I got in my car and went home. And waited.

CHAPTER 24

I was staring at the pictures when Judge Beck came down the steps. Yoga with Daisy had been less than relaxing, and I was running on three hours of very uneasy sleep.

Mayor Briscane. I could hardly believe it. He was pleasant, good humored, happily married, with a troubled son—a son he did everything he could to help. Mayor Pete Briscane had a secret. He liked something that would ruin his career and his marriage if it got out. And now, it would more than ruin his career, it would send him to jail.

I knew what happened, but I didn't have the sort of proof that sent a man to jail. I had the word of a woman that a girl long dead had told her that the one who most likely killed her wasn't a teen boy but a grown man. I'd connected the dots to the only person who that could be, the only person David Briscane would take the fall for. And I had this picture of Mayor Briscane, waiting by the parked big rigs behind the truck stop.

It was all so circumstantial. Pete could just say he feared it was David and wanted to hear what I knew, so he could know for himself if his son was guilty of premeditated murder. Sheila could be discredited as not remembering what Desiree had said years ago, or getting the guys confused, or that Desiree had lied. The black book was full of indecipherable codes. And Sydney wouldn't testify that Caryn was providing kinky sex to someone who paid her a whole lot of money to strangle her during the act.

"What, no muffins this morning?" Judge Beck teased. He was wearing plaid pajama pants again with a white t-shirt, his hair mussed and the shadow of whiskers on his face. I'd heard him come in after midnight last night and was surprised to see him up so early.

"No, I had a late night working. I did make coffee, though. Help yourself."

He disappeared into the kitchen and came back with a mug and the coffee pot to top mine off.

"Is that Pete?" He looked closer at the picture that I'd transferred from my phone to the computer screen. "At the truck stop? At night?"

I nodded. "I got a note at work yesterday, stuck in the door. Here." I handed it to him.

He read it, then looked back at the screen. "And you called the mayor rather than the police? Is he investigating this case now?"

I told him the whole thing, from Sydney to Sheila to Trip's late-night surveillance. The judge listened, then scratched his cheek.

"None of this will hold up in court, you know?"

"I know." I looked up at him. "Do you believe me, though? I can't imagine Pete Briscane doing something like this, but it's the only thing that makes sense. And he showed up at the truck stop last night."

"It's a valid theory, but there are a million loopholes, a million chances for the defense to plant reasonable doubt.

There needs to be more. There needs to be someone who knew what he was doing, to link him to the sex act and the prostitution ring. Caryn can't have been his only partner in the last ten years. The police will just need to turn up another witness to connect him. And possibly they'll be able to figure out the code in the black book, or find evidence of Pete being at Caryn's or something."

"He has to be feeling the heat," I mused. "Otherwise why write the note and take the risk of coming to meet me?"

"Because J.T. told him and he wanted to pay you off to keep quiet about his son?" Judge Beck shrugged.

"He'd want to pay me off to keep quiet about a murderer?" Good grief, that was just as bad as him being the murderer himself. It was one thing to try to avoid gossip on a manslaughter charge, quite another to attempt to hush up premeditated murder.

"Maybe he doesn't think David is the killer, just that he's a client and in the black book."

That still didn't make sense. "Everyone in town knows David has been trouble. If it came out that he was the murderer, there's no one who would blame Pete for that. He's done everything for that boy. If anything, he'd gain a ton of sympathy votes. Everything I've uncovered, and my intuition, is telling me that Pete is the killer, that he's the one who killed Desiree Trottenhaus and paid his son to take the blame."

Judge Beck sat his coffee cup on my desk. "If that's true, Kay, then he's dangerous. Don't go any further with this. Take what you have to the police and wash your hands of the whole thing. If Pete has committed two first-degree murders, he won't hesitate to commit a third."

I chewed on my lip and thought. Pete had friends at the courthouse and in the police department. He was a great guy. No one would believe any of this, and while they'd investigate it, in the meantime I was willing to bet there would never be enough for an arrest, let alone a conviction. One girl's "I was told" from years ago, an indecipherable black book, a prostitute that wouldn't come forward, a few cell phone pics of the mayor by the truck stop. It wasn't enough.

"Okay. Let me get a shower and we'll go. I can see you're not going to let this drop, and I'm honestly afraid for you, Kay."

I looked up at him in surprise. "Go where?"

"To Stenburg to get some barbeque for lunch."

CHAPTER 25

*B*riscane's BBQ wasn't the shack I'd assumed. The place was the size of most big chain restaurants with three pool tables off from the bar and motorcycle-themed décor covering the walls. Blues music barely drowned out the murmur of conversation. We had to wait for a table, and I nearly died of starvation hovering by the hostess station smelling smoked pork and brisket.

How much money had Pete given his son? College, and this? I'd just assumed ten or twenty grand to cover some start-up costs, but opening a place of this size had to have cost more than a mansion. Pete and his wife must have nearly bankrupted themselves to set this up—all for a troubled son who had multiple run-ins with the law, and was kicked out of college.

And David was having financial difficulties from the case search I'd done on him. This place looked successful, so either the money was going elsewhere, David was a poor manager of his finances, or he was just really lazy about paying his bills.

I ordered a pulled pork sandwich and Judge Beck got the

sliced beef. It came on huge plates with fries, coleslaw, and a bowl of baked beans. The waitress plopped a basket of corn bread down and refilled our ice tea as I dug in.

Holy cow, it was good. Judge Beck asked the waitress if David was in while I shoveled down the food with unseemly haste. The pork had a vinegar bite and a mustardy sauce, all held together by a thick potato roll. The fries had been beer-battered, and the coleslaw had the perfect mix of sweet and tangy flavor. But it was the cornbread that had me thinking of recipes. Moist and dense like a cake, it had a sweet flavor and bits of corn throughout. I could make this. And then maybe do a drier batch with cheese and jalapeño to have with chili. I wondered if the kids liked chili. Did Judge Beck like chili?

We were finished with our meal and sipping tea by the time David Briscane came over to our table. He pulled over a chair and turned it around to straddle it, giving us a warm, genuine smile.

"It's good to see folks from Locust Point here. I haven't been back home in years. Mrs. Carrera, I know you don't know me, but your husband coached our Little League team when I was eight. I'm so sorry to hear of his passing."

I hadn't been expecting this huge, popular establishment, and I hadn't been expecting Pete's reprobate son to be so polite and friendly. But then again, Pete didn't seem like a murderer, either.

Judge Beck introduced himself then nodded for me to take over. David shot me a frown before I could even speak. "Is this an intervention? Because I'm in A.A. now. I can put you in touch with my sponsor. I haven't missed a meeting in the last thirty days."

"It's a different kind of intervention," I told him. "I work for J.T. Pierson doing skip tracing, and Caryn Swanson was one of our bail clients."

David squirmed on the chair, looking down at his hands. "I heard she was killed."

I decided to cut right to the heart of the matter rather than drag this out. "She was killed by a client who didn't want to be exposed through the course of her trial, someone who paid her to cater to his desire to perform asphyxiation during sex."

His jaw clamped tight. "And you're here because in spite of juvenile records being sealed, you discovered what happened with Desiree, and automatically think I'm Caryn Swanson's client and murderer."

"No, I think your father is the client and the murderer." There was that cutting to the heart of the matter again.

It was like every muscle in David's body seized up for a moment, then he let out a long breath. "What happened with Desiree back then was an accident. We were playing around with kinky stuff we'd found on the internet and took it too far. I confessed."

I noticed he didn't say anything in defense of his father. "Pete came to you and asked you to confess. The jury wouldn't have gone easy on him. They never would have believed it was an accident. He would have been convicted of second degree murder, branded a pedophile. His career and marriage would have been ruined, and he would have served jail time. You were a minor. You could throw yourself on the mercy of the court and they'd most likely give you a light sentence, which would be sealed. You didn't want to see your dad in jail, your family ruined, and Pete offered a significant financial incentive."

"I confessed," David repeated. "I was given probation. It's over. You can speculate all you want, but I was pronounced guilty of involuntary manslaughter. It's done."

"Is it?" Judge Beck asked. "You said you hadn't been back to Locust Point for years, but your father said you were there last weekend, no doubt to ask for more money. Are you holding Desiree's death over his head? Continuing to drain money from your father or you'll let everyone know what really happened?"

I had no idea what Judge Beck was doing until I saw the spark of anger in David's eyes.

"I haven't asked that man for a dime for ten years. He summoned me. He's the one who asked me to come home that weekend. I thought maybe Mom was ill. I never expected..."

"Never expected that he'd ask you to take the fall for another murder?" I asked softly. "Did he tell you that he'd been a client of Caryn Swanson's, that his name was in that black book? Did he tell you he was worried she'd tell exactly what he liked to do as part of her plea bargain, and that his career would be over? Did he tell you if Caryn went public with what he liked to do, someone was bound to connect the dots to Desiree's murder ten years ago?"

David shook his head and stood. "Look, it's nice you all came out here, but you're wrong."

"You sure?" Judge Beck asked. "You know you're a prime suspect, David. You'll take the fall for this one whether you want to or not. The Briscane in that black book, the kink, your past conviction. And this time you'll go to jail for the rest of your life. This wasn't involuntary manslaughter; it was first degree murder. It was premeditated, and you'll once again pay the price for your father's mistakes."

The man caught his breath, then slowly sat back down. "When I went home last weekend, he told me that Caryn had been killed, that he'd been a client of hers and because of how she kept her records, everyone would think it was me. He wanted me to flee the country, was going to give me money to go to Mexico. I thought...I thought maybe he was truly worried about me being falsely accused and going to jail."

"But you didn't go," I prompted him.

"No. I was so angry that after what happened before he had continued to pay women to let him do *that*. He hadn't learned his lesson, even after he accidently killed Desiree. But it wasn't just that. I've made a life here. I have a successful business, a girlfriend. I've had issues, but I'm in treatment and I'm turning things around. I'd rather take my chances with the court system and have faith that I'd be proven innocent, than leave everything I've built behind to run away."

It still wasn't enough. David could testify that it was his father who killed Desiree, but there was nothing here to tie him to Caryn Swanson's murder. All I had was proof that Pete had a kink. He had motive, but I was sure lots of her clients had motive.

"You were home last weekend?" Judge Beck asked. "When did you speak with your father?"

David frowned a minute. "Saturday afternoon. I got in late Friday after we closed here, and I didn't see him until around noon Saturday."

I hadn't found Caryn Swanson's body until Tuesday. This proved Pete Briscane was our killer. The judge shot me a quick warning glance.

"We might need you to testify, David."

The man swallowed hard, then nodded. "Okay. It's his own fault. If he'd just learned his lesson, he wouldn't be facing this scandal. But just because my dad does this stuff doesn't mean he's a killer. What happened with Desiree was an accident. He's not the kind of guy who'd kill in cold blood. Not Dad."

We paid our bill and left, remaining silent until we were in the car and on the freeway.

"Remind me never to play poker with you," I told Judge Beck. "You can bluff like a pro."

"Likewise. And you do realize that the only concrete thing we have is David's word that Pete knew of Caryn's death before her body had been discovered?"

I nodded. "Will David be a reliable enough witness to make a murder charge stick?"

The judge shook his head. "There's a whole lot of coincidence, then the word of a man who has been in his share of trouble. Pete will just say he's lying, and between the pair of them, the mayor is the most believable. We'll go talk to the detective in charge of the case, but he's going to need to get more than this before they even think of charging Pete."

I sighed, wondering if our mayor was going to get away with this murder just as he'd done with Desiree's. How could I ever see him in J.T.'s office, at the regatta or other events, knowing what I knew?

"Patience, Kay," Judge Beck said. "Leave it up to the detective, and have faith that justice will prevail. You've dug the fox out of his den. Now let one of the bigger dogs take him down."

Sometimes the bigger dogs didn't fit in the fox-hole. Sometimes you needed a terrier to finish the job. But I wasn't that terrier. Judge Beck was right. I'd been in over my head for days on this case. It was time to step aside.

"Okay, you win. Time to send in the big dogs."

$\mathcal{I}$ spent the rest of the weekend trying to knit a reasonably functional washcloth, planning out a small vegetable garden, reading, and trying not to think about Caryn Swanson, or Pete Briscane. It was difficult with Daisy wanting to discuss the case every morning after yoga. I kept my mouth shut, though, and filled the hours with as much as I could.

True to his word, Judge Beck took Madison shopping on Sunday afternoon. The poor guy looked like he was ready for a bottle of whisky when they came through the doors, arms laden with shopping bags. Madison modeled several dresses and what seemed like a hundred shirts and skirts. Then I was treated to a preview of an eyeshadow palette and some pencil that was supposed to make her eyebrows "on-fleek," whatever that meant.

I loved it. And Judge Beck obviously did too, even though he'd clearly had his fill of teen fashion and makeup. When her mom honked outside to pick her up, Madison practically bounced with excitement. She grabbed the bags and was halfway to the door before turning around and rushing into her father's arms.

"Thank you, Daddy. I love you."

"I love you too, Maddy."

I saw his face as his daughter hugged him, saw his expression as he said the words back, as he waved and watched her leave. Then I saw his face as he turned and went up the stairs to his bedroom. He loved his kids. I was pretty sure he still loved Heather. And this whole thing was like a knife tearing through his chest.

On Monday morning I was back at my desk, once again wading my way through Creditcorp files and two background-checks for bail requests. J.T. was late, but that wasn't unusual on a Monday morning. He often ran by the courthouse on his way in, or met with potential clients. By ten o'clock I could resist no longer. I set aside the folders and once again logged onto Caryn Swanson's social media accounts, digging up pictures from six months back and earlier. There was nothing there beyond pictures from her company's events, some vacation pictures, a few family shots, and selfies.

But one of the selfies caught my eye. It was one of those horrible bathroom-pics taken in the mirror, but instead of seeing a toilet or dirty tub in the background, the picture showed an open doorway into what looked to be a bedroom.

And there, standing in front of the bed, shirtless and easing down his pants was a man. I caught my breath and enlarged the photo, hoping it was who I thought.

Pete Briscane. This was proof that he was having sex with Caryn if not a client. Perhaps this, plus all the other circumstantial evidence and David's testimony, would add up to enough. Perhaps.

The bell chimed and I looked up with a smile on my face

to greet my boss. It wasn't J.T. walking over to me as I sat in front of the computer. It was our mayor.

His eyes flicked to the screen on my computer and narrowed. "Missed seeing you at the truck stop, Kay."

My heart felt like it was about ready to fly out of my chest. He was blocking my only exit. There was no way I could get to a phone before he tackled me, and the guy had a good seventy pounds on me. Plus, he was skilled at strangling women. I, on the other hand, was not skilled at escaping murderers.

But it seemed strangling wasn't what he had in mind. Pete pulled a pistol from his jacket pocket and flicked off the safety.

"J.T. will be here any minute," I told him.

"No, he won't. He's meeting me for brunch. I'll take care of you, go have French toast with my friend, then be as shocked and horrified as he is when he finds your dead body."

"David told us," I said, desperate to stall long enough to think of a way out of this. Could I somehow manage to go all Hulk, tip over the desk and use it as a shield? Could I throw a pencil and manage to hit him in the eye? "David told Judge Beck and me everything. I'm not the only one who knows. We know about Desiree, about your fetish, about how you were a client of Caryn's."

He shrugged. "There's no evidence. And the detectives in our illustrious small-town police force? They couldn't investigate their way out of a paper bag. You're the only one putting the pieces together, Kay. I need to make sure you don't dig up enough to make this a problem for me. The case needs to die, and so do you."

I gritted my teeth, posed to rush him, when the door chimed. There was that second where it seemed time stopped. Pete's eyes shifted to the door. I dove under the desk. And a burly guy with head-stubble and cowboy boots tackled the mayor.

The gun went off. J.T. threw an amazing right hook, and before I could crawl out from under the desk, my boss had the gun. Pete was facedown on the floor, his arm twisted behind him, J.T.'s knee on his back. I dialed 911, and because the courthouse was right across the street, we had half a dozen police in our office within seconds.

Pete was hauled off in cuffs, the gun bagged and tagged, statements taken, and I found myself staring at a bullet hole in our office wall and my computer screen with a picture of a half-naked Pete Briscane behind and to the right of Caryn Swanson in a hotel room.

That's when I started to shake, my knees buckling. Thankfully, my office chair was right behind me.

"You okay, Kay?" J.T. asked.

He was flushed, eyes shining with excitement. I thought he'd be shocked and horrified over the arrest of one of his friends, but that wasn't the case. I figured out why from what he said next.

"Did you get any video of that? Did anyone get video of that? Did you see me? Now that's reality show stuff, right there. Snake doesn't tackle politicians who are trying to kill his assistant. If nobody got video, I'll need to do a recreation. Do you think that would work? We could flash *recreated* on the screen. Yes. That way I can make sure my head is freshly shaven and I've got a cowboy belt on."

J.T. I loved the guy. He'd saved my life, and if he wanted me to hold a video camera while he tackled an actor portraying Pete Briscane, I would absolutely do it.

"It is reality show stuff, J.T. This whole week has been an episode of *Snake, Bounty Hunter*."

My boss's chest puffed out. "That's *Pierson, Bounty Hunter*."

CHAPTER 27

*N*ews spreads fast in a little town like Locust Point. I came home to find Daisy camped out on my doorstep, a bottle of wine and two glasses in her hand.

"Good grief, Kay. I don't know what shocked me more, that Pete Briscane is a murderer, or that he almost shot you dead right in your office."

It sounded ridiculously dramatic, but that's what happened. Maybe J.T. was right and we did have the makings of a good reality television show, or at the very least, a Lifetime special movie.

"I'm just glad J.T. stopped by the office to grab some files," I told her as I opened the door.

She shook her head. "J.T. Pierson, action hero. Who would have thought it? That's one more thing that shocks me. The day is full of unbelievable events. Next thing you'll tell me that Taco is penning a bestseller and Judge Beck is going to pole dance in his underwear for my birthday."

Once again Daisy's imagination had flown to the next state. "I think three unbelievable events in one week is enough."

She poured a glass of wine and handed it to me. "My birthday isn't for three weeks, so I'm still holding out hope for Judge Beck in his underwear."

We drank our wine, and I started to feel less like an almost-murder-victim. By the time Judge Beck and the kids came home, I was nearly back to normal. Once again, I had to go over the whole story, with Henry, Madison, and Daisy acting out the roles in my living room. The judge declared it was a good night for pizza, and we all sat at my dining room table and ate.

After the last slice of four-cheese had been eaten, the kids went upstairs to do their homework. We all stayed and chatted, Judge Beck joining us in a glass of wine. Eventually he made his way upstairs, and soon after, Daisy left with the empty wine bottle to her home, leaving me alone.

But I wasn't alone. I had good friends. I had a boss that had tackled and disarmed a killer. I had a roommate and his two kids that were fast becoming like a family to me. I had my beloved Taco. And I had my shadowy floater friend who was back, hovering just out of view in the corner of the dining room. This new stage in my life seemed less scary. In fact, this new stage in my life seemed like it was turning into something grand.

I picked up Taco and headed toward the stairs down to the television room. Rom Com? Why yes, I thought it was an excellent night for romantic comedy. Glancing out of the corner of my eye at the shadow, I jerked my head.

"Come on. You too. If you're lucky, I might even let you pick the movie tonight."

FOR MORE KAY CARRERA, grab Junkyard Man, A Locust Point Mystery #2

ACKNOWLEDGMENTS

Special thanks to Lyndsey Lewellen for cover design and typography, and to Erin Zarro for copyediting.

ABOUT THE AUTHOR

Libby Howard lives in a little house in the woods with her sons and two exuberant bloodhounds. She occasionally knits, occasionally bakes, and occasionally manages to do a load of laundry. Most of her writing is done in a bar where she can combine work with people-watching, a decent micro-brew, and a plate of Old Bay wings.

For more information:
libbyhowardauthor@gmail.com

ALSO BY LIBBY HOWARD

Locust Point Mystery Series:

The Tell All

Junkyard Man

Antique Secrets

Hometown Hero (November 2017)

A Literary Scandal (January 2018)

CPSIA information can be obtained
at www.ICGtesting.com
Printed in the USA
BVHW082333091219
566160BV00001B/150/P

9 781733 069106